LOVE TRIALS

JEAN GOULBOURNE

CONTENTS

1

AUNTIE MAG

Auntie Mag put the white drill trousers on the scrub board and began to push it against the ridges. Long Dan's clothes must be crisp and clean for church Sunday morning. She had to get the dirt out, all of it. It had rained last week and Long Dan had walked in the mud to come home. She had gone to church too and she had seen how dirty the church flooring was after the congregation had stepped in with the mud on their shoes. She cleaned the church floor every Friday and she sighed as the thought of the job. But she loved doing it as much as she loved washing Long Dan's clothes.

Long Dan her secret love.

A great man that. He was tall just like the giraffe she had once seen in a child's reading book and he was single and alone. She cooked his meals for him, kept house washed and ironed his clothes. All she needed now was the ring and the sacred place in his bed. It had been ten years of trying to attract him but not yet not yet. Maybe the time was not right and as she waited like a secret lover on her man she endured the pain of waiting as she imagined the time he would pop the question to her on his knees with the engagement ring in his hands putting it on her fingers then the bridal march some time afterwards with the song 'Here comes the bride' being played by the church organist as she walked up to join him at the altar. Wait wait wait. It was painful to have to wait while so many younger women had done it had eased themselves into the heart of some man and captured his attention. But Long Dan was a stubborn old mule and Auntie Mag was growing old now. Time was fleeting like a high wind and still she waited.

While she waited she prayed just as Hannah had done silently at the altar every Friday after cleaning the church floor and arranging the flowers and the various pieces of worship on the altar place before the Minister. Sometimes she took a candle with her, lighted it and prayed. She was alone in the huge building and no one seemed to know her secret except the Creator and she knew that she would wait on Him to tell her when it would be time for Long Dan to propose, marry her and take her on a honeymoon and give her nice clothes and shoes. For Auntie Mag was poor as a church mouse and depended on the pittance from cleaning the church and keeping house for Long Dan for a living.

Auntie Mag smiled. Yeah man, she would wait for that glorious day, that unforgettable experience, when she would grace the dining table as lady of the house, full of pride for what she had put on the table for the both of them and later for the children that would come for although she was in her late thirties, she longed for the little smile and the tiny hands of a child, holding her captive in love.

When Auntie Mag was ready with the drill suit she hung it on the clothes line. She hoped there would be no rain today. That would be a disaster, Long Dan had to wear his suit this Sunday and she would watch him walk up the aisle collecting money in the collection plate and feel proud as she sat on the choir. Yes, she sang alto on the church choir, did Auntie Mag. They had practiced the hymns they would sing that Sunday morning on Tuesday evening choir practice and Pastor was pleased as punch as he sat there in the first pew below the altar and listened to the choir master, who was the local headmaster of the school, sing the songs with the choir.

With the clothes on the clothes line facing the morning sun, Auntie Mag went into the house to finish the cleaning and to prepare Long Dan's evening meal which she would place carefully on the table under cover from the flies. She would eat something and go home to return in the evening to take the dried suit and iron it with the flat iron that she heated on the coal fire that she cooked on.

She entered the bedroom to straighten the place as she did every morning. She looked at the bed. It was a four poster from way back in time maybe from Long Dan's grandmother's time and she had already put a spread on it. It was a blue chenille bed spread. Auntie Mag smiled. How she longed to lie in that bed with her husband beside her. Her husband Dan. Time will tell. Nothing happens before its time the good book said. She must wait.

The dresser was dusty so she found the duster and began to clean it. Where did all the dust come from she wondered as she grabbed the duster. It was then that she saw the letter on the dresser. It was opened flat out on the wooden surface. How could she help but read it?

"My beloved Dan" it began. Tears gathered as she read the piece of romance that the letter represented. It came from a woman in St Bess, the parish of her grandparents, parents who had both died long ago. She wanted to tear the missive to bits but resisted the temptation. She read the letter slowly. This was real romance. This was a real love letter. She finished reading and looked up at the mirror that was on the dresser, she felt that she could see the woman in the glass.

"Just you wait," she muttered to her "you wait, I will get you even if is a obeah man I have to go to. Lord Jesus Help me. Long Dan have a girl friend and is not me. You forget me Lord, Why? When me clean you church and wash the Pastor surplice? When me sing on the choir and try to make sure the girl children wear hat to cover them sins? Me Lord? Me who pray like Hannah for a child within a marriage to Dan? Me, your servant Maggie better known as Auntie Mag?

First it was disbelief. Dan would never hurt her, would he? Maybe the woman Ruby was an admirer that Dan would never want. Maybe it was another Dan and he had got hold of this letter from the other Dan. Maybe it was a ruse to make her jealous or why would he leave the letter open like that? Just maybe, maybe, maybe till it hit her that the maybes did not matter. It was true. This was why Long Dan had disappeared sometimes saying he was going on business. He was going to St Bess. But why lie to her? Why? She had never let him know her feelings for him. She had hidden it under her tie head like a sacred secret. She had been as professional as any helper can be. Why Why Why? She began to shed tears but they did not bring relief. They accompanied the deep feeling to hate for the famous Ruby and the feeling of revenge. She would kill her if she ever came into this house. She would use cassava poison and kill her. No one would ever know. Then Long Dan would see her and know her as he should. He would be her husband. Auntie Mag began to plan.

Auntie left the dresser with the dust and placed the letter back where she had found it. Anger deepened into bitterness. Everybody and everything was against her. She had to be a domestic servant all her life. Why did God allow this to happen? He, who she worshipped and cared so much about? He whose church floor she cleaned and whose church building she kept spotless? What was God's plan for her? She wished she could die. But no she would kill Ruby. Ruby would die for this. Dan was hers, had always been hers and she would begin to take her secret from under her tie head and flaunt it in his face. You just watch and see.

After finishing her work in the house, Auntie Mag started on her journey home. She had a mile to walk on the main road and then down through a lonely pathway to her house in a valley far away from the main road. She was lonely there, so lonely sometimes that she would go and hold a one sided conversation with the goats. There were five of them, and aside from the old broken down hovel in which she lived, and the two surrounding acres her parents had left her, they were her only investment. She would sell a goat when she was in dire need.

On her journey, she met Mad Ants and Tall Blacks, two young men from the district next to hers. She was too angry to answer their "Evening, Auntie Mag". She brushed past them with a face that was full of hate. She had decided that she hated all men.

"Auntie Mag vex like bull today," said Mad Ants who was as cool as a cucumber despite his name.

"I wonder is what hurt her now." said Tall Blacks.

"Maybe somebody in the church or Long Dan. Me really want to know because she never always behave like that." said Mad Ants.

The two young man walked down the road towards the square. They saw Long Dan coming up the road towards them.

"Evening Mass Dan, " they chorused.

"Evening, how you do?" Long Dan replied.

"We alright. But Auntie Mag not so alright. Is what happen to her?" asked Mad Ants

"Auntie Mag? Me nuh know maybe is the time of month again. You never know." replied Long Dan laughing.

"Maybe. You never know with woman." said Tall Blacks who had a troublesome girlfriend.

"Anyway me going home to me dinner. I only hope she cook something nice for me" said Long Dan going up the road to his house.

"Alright." The young men chorused to Long Dan as they went their way. They were going to the local bar

Long Dan passed the pimento trees and the slim bamboo plants that lined the roadside. The road was unpaved and the dust flew up when the cars passed. The dust was bauxite red. But there were just a few cars in the district and only few cars passed through to go to the south of St Bess. The countryside was quiet. There were only a few things happening to make news. The newspapers came in only for the teacher at the school and the pastors of the churches in the district. The radio was only in a few homes and some who owned them kept them on for only an hour or two in the evenings to preserve the batteries. Electricity had not yet come to the district. Crime was almost non- existent and the few times that anything resembling crime was reported to the local police, it was theft of a few goats or stealing of crops from the field of some farmer. Break-ins were not common and the perpetrators were likely to be punished by the locals with a whipping. The policemen were bored and laid back. They had so little to do.

The evening passed into night and all three men forgot about Auntie Mag and her troubles while Auntie Mag took in the goats from the bush around the house and put them in a pen and went inside to bed without supper. She bathed in cold water from the tank in the yard and schemed as she took the bath. She had to know what to do. But in spite of her scheming she felt as helpless as a young ram goat ready for the knife.

She cried all night.

2

LONG DAN

When Long Dan arrived home, he went to the kitchen removed his meal from the kitchen table and went to the dining room with it. He removed the cover. It was his favourite, cabbage and codfish. He ate with relish. It was good. Auntie Mag was such a good cook. He knew Ruby could cook but she was in the family way two months now and he wanted to make things easy for her now that she was carrying his child. So yes, he would keep Auntie Mag as the helper till the child was born and maybe afterwards too. She would help Ruby settle in and take care of the child when they had to be away from the house.

Somewhat vaguely, he wondered what was troubling Auntie Mag. She was always such a happy person and she was devoted to her job. He knew that. But then he thought of Ruby and the coming baby and that put Mag completely out of his mind. As he ate, he thought of the many tomorrows that lay ahead for them, the wedding that they were planning, the birth of the child and then more children if possible.

He worked as a tax collector and he had his gardens in which he grew a few food crops for himself and for sale to the higglers when they came around. He had five acres of land and Ruby was anxious to get into the chicken business that was taking over the place. She wanted layers that would provide additional income for themselves and the baby.

Ruby came from a farming family in St Bess and was accustomed to life on a farm where they grew scallion , thyme, cassava and many other crops suited for the dry climate. He was glad to have met her and be successful in his courtship. He had waited for so long for this and she was right for him. He was sure of that.

After eating, he went back to the kitchen and washed the dish. Then he went to his bedroom. He saw the letter on the dresser and wondered how he could have left it out like that. He smiled. Auntie Mag was a prying one and he was sure that she read it. The news would be over the district in no time. Never mind. It was not bad news. He was happy and that was enough for him. He was sure that the men at the rum bar and the grocery shop would be clapping him on the back and congratulating him now. They had teased him for long enough. Now was his turn to take the back slapping and the occasional drink from the bar.

Long Dan sat back in his chair by the window and contemplated life. He was incredibly happy. His lonely life was going to change soon. He had called on Pastor Granger to ask him to announce the wedding bans in church. His and Ruby's would be a small wedding. Just a few of their friends and relatives. He would give the best speech at the wedding and he was already preparing it. Long Dan was fairly well educated, as he had passed the Third Jamaica Local examination at an early age and had become a tax collector after serving in the Parish Council in the nearby town. He knew that many of the younger women had been after him but he had not been really interested. Ruby had attracted him from the first glance. She was pretty and plump just as he liked them and she had returned the interest he had in her. Life was looking up. She would get the five acres working even harder by employing local people to help him, something he had never been able to do much with as he was so involved in his work. His work took him all over the parish and into town a lot.

The wedding would take place in the church right there in the district and the reception was to be held in the schoolroom. He had already arranged all of that. Ruby's family was coming up to prepare and arrange for the food. They had to have a goat killed for curried goat and some chickens to fry There had to be mannish water as well. He thought of buying the ram goat from Auntie Mag. He had to help the poor lady as she was really pathetic living there in the bushes with the goats and the few chickens. He wondered sometimes just how she managed. She would welcome the sale of that ram goat. No celebration took place in the district without curried goat and white rice and goat head soup or mannish water as it was known . Maybe Auntie Mag would help to cook the meal. She would be glad for such a job. She had cooked at celebrations in the past.

Long Dan had already arranged to get a new suit. He had bought the material and given it to the tailor in town. Ruby decided to get her wedding dress in the city. The wedding was to be in a month's time as Ruby did not want anyone to know yet that she was already pregnant. The speculations would come later. He was prepared for that. He just wanted to see his love settled and happy before the birth of his first child. Just think of it, a little baby in the house. He hoped it would be a boy to begin the crop of children because he wanted many children even if it meant building another room or two on the house.

Long Dan stood and looked out the window and decided to get a drink at the bar. He wondered if Mag had spread the news already. She was a strange one, was Mag. What on earth was she on about with Mad Ants and Tall Blacks? Those were two young men who wouldn't hurt a fly let alone Auntie Mag. Long Dan chuckled as he contemplated this and he went to the door pulled the latch and went outside. He must face the back slapping and the teasing if Auntie Mag had done as she always did, spread news just like Miss Tiny the telegram woman who knew every tragedy and every sickness before the telegram receiver.' Lord help me' he said to himself and he chuckled again. Auntie Mag, what a character.

Long Dan went down the rough road, his long legs moving nonchalantly down the hill towards the village square. It was getting rather cool now. He had forgotten to take a pullover but he was accustomed to the cool air in the evening and indeed he relished it. Ruby's countryside in St Bess was hot and dry . He hoped that she would adjust to the cool air of South Manchester. There had not been much rain lately and the dust was high on the road banks. The few cars in the district made a fuss with the marl on the road. He disliked it that way. But it had always been like this. He wished that he would soon see asphalted roads in the areas around here. When when when he asked himself would such a thing happen. The mother country, Britain, was broke after the war and taxes from the colonies were slow in coming. He knew as a tax collector just how bad things were here and throughout the countries that Britain ruled. He met Miss Gatha coming up from the square and he met Mass Rob too. They greeted him.

Mass Rob stopped in the middle of the road. He was a short man so he looked up at Long Dan.

"Lawd Mass Dan, how the fields? The time getting dry you know."

"Yes Mass Rob, but what to do? The rains will come one day. We nuh have to just live and let live!"

"I tell you Mass Dan. We just have to pray. You going to church Sunday?

"As usual Mass Rob."

"But what a question. As if you ever miss a service. Well, take it easy and pray for rain. Hard times can be really hard around here. The water tank them soon run dry. We nuh want to carry water from parish tank again. That too hard. Well see you." And Mass Rob walked away

Miss Gatha had stood there listening hard. As soon as Mass Rob walked away she was ready to talk. "How you doing Mass Danny?" asked Miss Gatha. She was a small woman, black in complexion and inquisitive.

""Everything alright Miss Gatha." He answered her. "Things tough but I giving thanks"

"I tell you, what else we can do? The belly part still a go up and down. We need little rain though nuh true? It getting kinda dry. You nuh think so?" Miss Gatha obviously wanted a conversation and Long Dan wanted to get on down the road to the rum bar before it got really dark.

"The rain will come Miss Gatha," he said "The good Lord never give you more than we can bear. I tell you what. I rushing down the road. I have to see somebody before it get too dark." He dismissed her with a wave of his hand and hurried away. She stood watching him go down the road his long legs almost leaping down the lane. She had a frown on her face. Long Dan looked very happy and she wondered why.

The men in the rum bar wondered too at Long Dan's exuberance. He offered them a drink all around. That hardly happened. Maybe he got a raise or something. But no one mentioned the letter or Ruby or his forthcoming marriage. Long Dan walked away puzzled. It was late that night before he left the bar. Maybe Auntie Mag hadn't read the letter. He realised that she hadn't really dusted the dresser well. Maybe she didn't see it after all.

Anyway everyone would know what was what when Pastor Granger read out the bans on Sunday morning just after he, Long Dan, collected the church dues walked up the aisle with the collection plate and waited at the altar for the prayer of thanksgiving.

3
PASTOR GRANGER

Reverend Stephen Granger was up rather late that night. He was working on his sermon for Sunday. Ever since he had left his native Scotland and come to this country, he had chosen Thursdays to really work on the Sunday sermon. Stephen Granger was young enough, he was in his early forties and his wife, Lillian, in her late thirties. They had two children and they lived in the manse somewhere in the bushes, some distance away from the square and even further from the Presbyterian Church of which he was a pastor. Although he missed the Scotland of his youth, he loved this country. He loved the weather and the people and the sheer beauty of everything around him. Sometimes he would go into the hinterland and seek out the birds. He learnt the native names of birds like Auntie Katie, Canary and bald pate. He never took a catapult with him as he hated the way the birds were slaughtered for food.

It was here, in this country, that he had discovered other sources of food. The cassava, maize that the people called corn, yams, sweet potatoes, breadfruit avocado pears green and ripe bananas and so many other foods that were unknown to him in Scotland. He remembered the sameness of his diet in his home. Oats, bread, potatoes and so on, the diet was so limited but he had thought nothing of it till he came to this country. Could people really starve here? He thought not easily, even in a drought.

He thought about his sermon for Sunday. He had decided that it should be about Jesus' command that His people love one another. It was not a very difficult sermon to convey but it was such a difficult command to obey. It was hard to love the neighbour who hated you so much. It was hard to turn the other cheek. It was hard to look at wealth, see your own poverty and not hate the rich man in his castle. It was hard to be contented with a hovel of a home and twelve children as was the case of so many people around him. Yes, there was food but there was also poverty in the homes with too many children and no means of support but small insignificant parcels of land on which subsistence farming was done. The colonial government cared but little he realised even though he represented that government in a way. But what could he do? He was an insignificant cog in the wheel and he could not speak out for fear of losing his pittance from the church organisation of which he was a part. So he would preach, yes love one another and for Jesus' sake, turn the other cheek.

It was while he was preparing his desk and arranging the papers on it that he noticed a note from Mr Danville Johnson better known as Long Dan or Mass Dan. It mentioned the bans of marriage to someone from St Bess and he asked him to announce it on Sunday in church. Yes, Pastor remembered now that he had given him notice of the bans last Sunday after church. He was fond of Mass Dan as he called him. Mass Dan was a stalwart in the church. He was an elder and he helped to manage the purse strings and as a tax collector he was well suited for the job. Yes, so Mass Dan was tying the knot at last and early too. It seems he would have to conduct the wedding in that church on the hill himself. He was looking forward to it. He loved these country weddings and he was fond of curry goat and fried chicken even if he did not want to drink mannish water that all the other men seemed to love.

It was good that Mass Dan had decided to marry instead of having mistresses all over the parish with so many children that he could not afford to take care of them. He had seen that so many times and he had been distressed by it. It was one of the main causes of the poverty that prevailed in the country. There were too many children and too little money to take care of them. He longed to change that but even he, the pastor, could never change the culture of these people. They were too set in their ways.

He was happy that his two children went to a prep school in the town. They must never adopt the ways of these people. These people were not civilised. As soon as the children were old enough he would send them back home to attend school in Scotland or send them to a boarding school right here where civilised people attended. The school curriculum here was inadequate anyway and was geared towards keeping the people in their places, that is at the bottom of the ladder and although it occurred to him sometimes that that was unjust he could see no other way out. The people must never get out of their station in life. That was the law in his country undocumented though it was, and as a colony of Britain that had to be the law here too. Because let's face it, these people were somehow less that the average Scots man, their very speech indicated that. Gibberish that was what they spoke and he was determined never to have his own children speak that way. Heaven forbid that he should hear one word of the gibberish spoken in his household except among the maid or gardener amongst themselves.

Pastor Granger sat down on his straight backed chair. His life here was fairly easy. He preached just once a week and the locals assisted him sometimes. The schoolmaster sometimes took over when he asked him to and he slept late in the weekdays and visited the sick from the congregation when there was any serious illness. He held a special place in the hearts of the villagers he knew as he represented the colonial power and therefore he was somewhat feared and respected. He also controlled some matters in the local schools as he was the manager and could dismiss the principal and other teachers and he could withhold their pay if anything went wrong. It was a good life for him and his children and he couldn't help wondering how he would fit into life in Scotland again his he had to.

Oh well he said to himself as he sat down pen in hand. He had to write this sermon. So get to it. There was silence except for the call of the birds in the garden and the occasional bark of a dog as he got his sermon under way. Love one another.

4
RUBY

Ruby hugged herself around the waist. She was so happy, a baby was on the way. She remembered the nights with the two latest men in her life and had decided to tell Dan that it was his child even though she couldn't be sure. Delroy didn't want another child to care for, he already had seven with three other women. Dan now, had none and he was glad to accept this one even if it was not his own. If only Danny knew. If only he knew that she was known as a wild tempestuous woman who had had many men. But Danny was a churchman, a man who respected the ways of the Christian church and in a way she was glad for that, maybe now she would settle and be at peace. Because she wanted that peace and maybe being away from her district in St Bess, in a place where she was not known, would help to calm her down.

What will it be like? She wondered about being married to Dan in a strange district among strangers and being forced by obedience to attend a church, something she had not done since she was a child?

She was not sure she liked the idea of obedience though. She was self -willed and determined to have her own way. Dan was a strong willed man too. Could two bulls reign in one pen as her mother use to say to her when she defied her? Well for the sake of peace, she would try till the baby was a little older then she would see if she could truly be the obedient wife.

Ruby frowned. Wonder of Dan had other women? He was in his thirties. Could he have been with many women? It was unusual for a man of his age and stature to be alone for so long. Never mind, she would find out and deal with the women as only she knew how.

As she sat on the four poster bed into which she had been born she remembered the two occasions when she had aborted the babies. Her mother had been horrified. But Ruby was never sure of the fathers and she knew that the men she had slept with would deny that it was theirs. In spite of her behaviour, Ruby craved decency. She was not a prostitute and she did not take money for her favours except when she was in desperate need. Her parents had tried with her and were in despair until Dan came along and they thought that at last she would settle down as a good man's wife at last. Ruby's mother was a Sunday school teacher and although her father only attended church about three or four times a year, he was also a believer and Ruby's behaviour had hurt them in the extreme.

Ruby's mother Celestina came into the room. She had a parcel in her hands. Ruby looked up expectantly.

"You uncle in foreign send this for you. You cousin carry it come " She said as she placed the brown paper parcel in Ruby's hands.

"Uncle Lue?" asked Ruby.

"Yes. Open it nuh!" said Celestina

Ruby opened the parcel slowly. In it was a sexy nightgown and a white sheet set. Ruby blushed.

"But see here!" exclaimed Celestina. "If you uncle ever knew. Put it away for your wedding night." She ordered her daughter.

Ruby got up and put the items away in her bottom drawer. Her mother was right. If Uncle Lue ever knew what she had been up to. Ruby had always been a favourite of her Uncle Lue who had gone overseas when she was still a child. For a while Ruby hid her face from her mother's perceptive eyes.

"So, you settling now girl?" asked Celestina, "No more wild life?"

"No more wild life Mama. I promise you. I changing for good."

"I hope so," her mother said as she left the room.

Ruby stood and went to the door of the bedroom and then out through the hall and onto the red dirt yard. There were chickens everywhere and their mess was scattered all about the hard earth. Her father had just come home from his scallion ground and was giving the donkey water from the water tank that stood somewhere down the yard. He looked up at her and then looked away and back at the donkey which was drinking steadily from the tin bucket at the side of the water tank's wall. It was a peaceful scene and Ruby had always loved this time of the evening. She smiled and said to herself that she would miss this.

She wondered if Dan would like to have as much land as her father or if he had enough money to buy more land. Farming was what Ruby knew best, having been brought up and reared in the food basket parish of St Bess. She was brought up on cassava and home made buns, milk from the cows and the goats, eggs from the chickens in the yard, good old gungu soup and meat seasoned with scallion and thyme from the gardens that her father tended.

She walked across the large hard dirt red yard towards the

thatched kitchen at the other end and marched into the cool interior. Esmie was standing in front of the fireside on which stood a huge three legged iron pot which was busy boiling away. Over the pot hung the creng creng with its meat for smoking. The smoke from the fire moved upwards and into the frail looking metal frame which held the meat.

"What you cooking Esmie?" asked Ruby as she went towards the fire and looked into the pot.

"Beef soup. Good," said Ruby answering her own question.

"How you feeling?" asked Esmie who was aware of Ruby's pregnancy.

"Good" answered Ruby hugging her stomach with her two hands.

"Looking forward to your wedding?" asked Esmie who had never married even though she had five boys now grown up and helping on the farm.

"Yes. And to a good man too."

"You must treat him good, you know. Him being a church elder and all."

"I telling you, Esmie I feel so proud. I never knew that he would want me you know. But I will try my best to treat him good."

"Glad to hear that. Well the soup soon ready. You can help me share?"

"Yes man, that way I will get plenty of it."

The two women laughed as they began to prepare the basins and the spoons. Ruby found the ladle and rinsed it in clean water. The family ate in the kitchen on benches at the side of the room. Eating in the house was for special occasions and visitors. Ruby and Esmie ladled the soup into the basins and Celestina walked in just as they were about to call the rest of the household in for the meal. The rest of the family entered and sat and slurped at the soup with the huge cartwheel cornmeal dumplings being chewed in between.

Ruby ate the rich beef soup and wondered just where life was leading her. She wondered if she loved Dan or whether this was a relationship based on convenience. Dan would accept this child as his own and she as making use of that. She knew that Dan loved her but she was not so sure that she retuned that love. As she ate she thought of ways she would try to make him happy. She could cook a rich beef soup just like this one and she could make bammies and homemade buns. She did a good stew too of meat and vegetables and she knew how to cook mannish water and curried goat.

Then she thought about her other talents in housekeeping. She knew how to keep a clean attractive house. It was part of her upbringing. The floor was spotless, cleaned and shining with the coconut brush and the bees wax. The curtains were kept washed and the furniture was also spotless dusted and rubbed down daily. She thanked her mother for that. She knew too how to wash and how to make sure that the iron after getting hot on the coal stove was scrubbed so that it would not dirty the clothes.

As Ruby ate the soup she hoped that Dan had someone to help her in the house. She knew that pregnancy meant that she had to slow down a bit and babies needed time and lots of care She would ask him when next she saw him. Ruby finished the soup and stood to collect the basins. It was her duty to wash the dishes that evening. Even though Esmie was the paid helper, Celestina made sure that Ruby did some of the work around the yard and in the house. Ruby smiled and remembered how she had often resented that rule. The knowledge she had gained from it was helpful to her now.

As the night approached that evening, Ruby sat around the

singer sewing machine and sewed the nappies made from terry cloth that she had bought recently in town. She had already sewed some clothes for the baby. Celestina sat on the bed nearby by and watched as the machine whirred away . They chatted late into the night.

5
SUNDAY MORNING

Sunday morning was sunny in South Manchester and there was a brisk breeze. Aunt Mag dressed with care putting on her white dress and white shoes and then she fastened her hat with a hat pin She had to look good. The talcum powder on her face covered the lines and the formation of wrinkles that had begun to show. She was growing old now she noted with distress but she had to look good for her beloved Mass Dan. She was prepared to fight for what she regarded as hers ,Mass Dan. She had no other prospects out there and she wanted to have a secure marriage and the benefit of a child. Child bearing years were slipping away. She wiped a tear that threatened to disfigure her face already thick with the talcum powder. She looked in the mirror and tried to smile, but her expression was grim.

"Jesus help me help me not to lose him. He means everything to me, everything. Help me not to hate even though I feel like killing Ruby when she comes to this district."

With that prayer on her lips, Aunt Mag fastened her door with a string. Nobody would steal from her meagre little house.

She glanced at her goats and they were fine then she marched up the uneven path from her home up the road to church that Sunday morning. Her steps were faster than usual and the look on her face was one of grim determination. She would still get him, she had to.

She walked pass the bamboo patch, pass the trees and shrubs red with the dirt from the roads where the cars had played havoc with the dust on the unpaved roads but Auntie Mag was not bothered by that. That was how it had always been for as long as she could remember and as long as she got what she wanted, Mass Dan, the roads could remain unpaved.

It was communion Sunday and the church was almost full by the time Mag arrived. Sunday school was over and the congregation was going to their seats. Mag joined the choir members on the platform and looked at her hymnbook and the Bible with unusual diligence. One young choir member giggled and Mag turned around and looked at her. The young lady shut up and looked down at her shoes. Auntie Mag had looked at her with a terrible glint in her eyes. The young lady stifled herself from the giggle and wondered what had happened to Auntie who had always been good to her. After the scraping of shoes and benches silence reigned. The pastor marched up the aisle with the elders and even the little children sat quietly. Mass Caleb was not ready to snore. That would come during the sermon and Mass Ivor was ready to sing in his tuneless voice as soon as the pastor announced the first hymn. Miss Erma looked down from her seat on the choir and noticed every child sitting down on the seats below her. She took it as her duty to berate every child who fidgeted or spoke during church services. The unfortunate child suffered from a lashing from the father or mother the next day.

They sang the first hymn. The Bible lessons were read and later the sermon was preached. Mass Caleb snored throughout

the sermon and the little children giggled into their handkerchiefs as they saw his open mouth. Mass Ivor sang with gusto
trying to outdo the choir and the pipe organ soared like an angel
over everything as Michie pumped the organ to life and the
organist swayed to the music as he played.

Long Dan then walked up to collect the collection plate and
went from seat to seat collecting pennies and three pennies and
sixpences. Pastor Granger looked anxious a he always did at that
time. There was only one paper money donation and it came
from the richest man in the district a Mr Keith. It was a five
shilling note. Then the march up to the alter for the prayer of
thanksgiving and Long Dan's long legs went back to the seat
where he sat to await Pastor Granger's announcement before
communion.

Pastor came to the very edge of the platform and he stood
awhile waiting for perfect silence. When silence reigned, he
began.

"I have been asked to announce the bans of marriage
between Mr Danville Johnson of this district to Miss Ruby Myers
of St Bess. May the union be blessed. Should anyone object to
this union speak now or hold your peace"

Silence reigned and then a murmur erupted into a volcano
as Auntie Mag stood from her seat and walked down the steps
towards Long Dan who was sitting in the second row. She
paused as she removed the hat pin from her hair then slowly
and deliberately flung the heavy hat into Long Dan's face and
hissed the word "Traitor" loud enough to be heard throughout
the whole church. She then walked down the aisle screaming
the word "Traitor."

Poor Long Dan could not move. He sat transfixed. His face
was a mixture a fear, consternation and bewilderment. He had
never seen this coming.

Then one small boy started to giggle and another child and

then another and the whole church burst into a roar of laughter that even the pastor joined in. Miss Erma roared forgetting the noisemakers and her self -assumed duty to keep the silence amongst the children in the church. The poor pastor knew there was hardly going to be a mood for communion that day. He held up his hand for silence and when the uproar had subsided he said the benediction and for the first time in the history of the church there was no communion on communion Sunday.

Long Dan stood and walked down the aisle as though hurrying to get away from the turmoil. The women wiped the tears of laughter from their eyes and the pastor wondered what would happen when this fiasco reached head office in the city. He had not controlled the church.

Auntie Mag marched up the road towards the path that would lead her to her little house tears streaming down her face like a flood. She paused to blow her nose in her best handkerchief and all she could say to herself was Traitor, Traitor.

She knew it would be the talk of the district for weeks if not months to come. Could she bear it?

When she arrived home she flung off her white shoes that were now smeared with the red bauxite dirt and fell into her bed onto the mattress that was filled with seymore grass and she sobbed herself trying to sleep. But she couldn't sleep.

It had happened. Her beloved was betrothed to another woman. She had lost him for good. Ruby. God Dammit . Ruby was her name. If she had her way Ruby would be stone dead by morning. But she did not know how to achieve that feat. It was too much, too much and too hard a burden to bear. She wanted to pray but could not. God had abandoned her. She no longer felt his presence with her and she had disgraced herself , she had let her feelings for Long Dan be known to the whole district.

Later she wondered why she had behaved like that. What about her job with Long Dan and the church cleaning, would she still be employed? But her thoughts gave way to anger and bitterness and after taking in the goats to their pen that evening and feeding the chickens and collecting the day's eggs she wandered through the hovel aimlessly. She felt as though she was going insane. No, she must not go mad ever, but she wanted Long Dan and she must have him. Tomorrow she knew, the news would rage about the district and beyond, but nine day wonders took care of themselves and this one would. She would deal with the rumours and the laughter behind the hands put to the smirking mouths . With that resolve she boiled some Sour Sop leaf tea changed into her night clothes went to bed and fell asleep.

6

LONG DAN

Long Dan spent a miserable afternoon and an even more miserable Sunday night. He was the laughing stock of the district. What if his beloved Ruby heard of his dilemma? What if she refused him now? Questions, questions tormented him and as he tossed and turned in his lonely bed his thoughts went from the sublime to the ridiculous. He even thought of killing himself, maybe drinking some pesticides or something like that. Maybe he needed to see a doctor of the mind and get some medicine. Maybe he should visit a balm yard and put a curse on Mag. He had been to balm yards as a child with his mother to help him make progress in school. But he was an elder in the church and that was now unthinkable. He got out of bed and knelt by his bedside and prayed. It had been years since he had prayed like this, kneeling by his bed.

Long Dan wondered how he would face the people in the district the following Monday morning. He had to go the work in the town and that meant taking the eight o clock bus in the village square with all those others who go to work in the town like himself. He could not hang his head in shame. His mother always told him to walk tall and so he would.

Then he started to ask God. Why Lord why? Why me? What have I done to deserve this, this curse? Who brought it on me? I have never touched Auntie Mag, she has only been my helper.

At about three o clock in the night, he slipped outside and picked some sour soup leaves from the tree in the yard. He made some tea with it and slept at last. It was a dreamless sleep. He woke at six o clock after a mere three hours of sleep and went to take a bath. As he washed himself he thought that maybe he ought to see the Pastor on his return from work in the evening. He needed to talk to somebody who would listen. He just needed someone who would be a friend. He realised that he had few friends in the district. Only a few that he could trust. He was rarely seen in the rum bars and he knew that many men considered him to be stand offish. He did little farming and had a job in the town. He sometimes went to the city on his work and he was educated, unlike so many of them in the area who depended on basic farming for their survival. Long Dan walked out of his house that morning and looked neither left nor right. Mad Ants and Tall Blacks saw him and looked at him with curiosity mingled with amusement but they said "Morning" as everyone said as a greeting in the district. "Morning" Long Dan replied his face long and his voice remote. He saw no one else as it was early and the children would not be going to school until nine o clock in the morning and farmers were probably in their grounds from much earlier. But the village square was full as people waited on the Morning Glory bus to come lumbering down the hill to settle and load. Dan stood aside. He did not mingle and there was nothing unusual about that as he had always been a loner. But some women looked at him with pity in the eyes and some men wanted to giggle but did not. They felt pity too but they knew that the shame would soon leave him as it was nothing but a nine day wonder. They wondered though about Ruby and how Auntie Mag came into the picture and what he would do next.

Long Dan boarded the bus when it came and took a seat at the very back. People climbed in and soon the bus was almost full. It would stop for people all along the way as it went on the twelve mile journey into the town then people would disembark and hurry to their jobs or to the shops. It was a familiar routine and Dan walked down the hill to his work place as soon as the bus entered the market square and came to a stop. He wanted no comments and for the time being he was safe. No one at work would be aware of what had happened at church yesterday.

All in all it was a quiet day at work. Dan pushed himself hard in order to forget. It was when he took the Morning Glory at five o clock that evening that it all came rushing back. He knew that Ruby would hear about it. What was he to do?. He came off at the village square and walked to the pastor's .Pastor would probably listen to him and that very thought that someone would listen without giggling or mocking him gave him solace. He walked with his long leg carrying him but he walked both with hope and a little fear. What if the Pastor refused to see him?. He feared going back home to his empty house with no food prepared and the place in the mess that he had left it in.

He arrived at the manse late in the evening and walked up the short driveway. A dog came leaping out at him. Long Dan stood and waited. He knew that the dog's barking would bring someone out. He didn't holler Hold dog as so many people would have done. The helper who lived there would understand but he wasn't sure about the pastor. He was not from this country. Sure enough the dog brought out the pastor. The pastor looked out and saw him he came down the driveway and ordered the dog called Rags to get back inside. Then he welcomed Long Dan and told him to come inside. The two men walked into the living room of the huge manse and then into the pastor's study. All that time hardly a word passed between them. They were both aware of the dilemma that faced Long Dan.

The two men sat down, the pastor indicating an easy chair while he went to a hard backed chair behind his desk which was covered with papers. They were quiet for a while as they faced each other. The pastor put his hand up in the praying position but he did not pray

"Well," said Pastor Granger breaking the silence, "I wonder what led to that outburst?"

"Pastor, I don't know. I didn't give that woman any encouragement. I had no idea that she felt that way about me. She was only my helper for God's sake. But to embarrass me like that right in the church in front of everybody, I feel I could strangle her."

"Don't give vent to your anger. It will only make matters worse. Maggie is lonely living there in the bushes with just the animals as friends. She must imagine things. Just remember that. It is hard to face the neighbourhood with all that on your mind but I suggest that you move the wedding from that church to the one in the town. I will ask the pastor there. You can have refreshments in the church hall. And maybe put off the wedding by a week or two so that things will calm down a bit.

"But what do I tell my intended? That that woman was after me and I did not know it? She is preparing for the wedding in a month's time."

"Tell her the truth. That's the best way"

Long Dan groaned. He had to face Ruby. He had to find himself to the district in St Bess and face the music.

"Just do it. It will make you more of a man. Hide the truth and it will stare you in the face down the line. Meanwhile forgive poor Maggie. She hid her feelings all this time. Be gentle with her. She might end up as a mental case if you are rough with her."

"You mean still employ her?"

"Maybe. You decide. But be firm. She is your helper. Not your lover."

"OK Pastor and thanks. I just needed someone to talk to."

"Anytime Mass Dan anytime."

The two men stood and shook hands then they walked through the living room and down the walkway.

Long Dan's long legs went down the road at a furious pace. He knew there would be no food in the house so he went to the shop and bought a tin of corned beef and some rice, then he thought of breakfast in the morning and he bought a tin of sardines and some bread. He knew that there was coffee in the tin at home. When he arrived at his house Long Dan was dead tired but he was also hungry. He washed his hands and prepared his meal thankful that his mother had taught him the rudiments of cooking. He ate quickly then drew water from the water tank for a cold bath He bathed and said a prayer of thanksgiving for the pastor and his advice. He slept well.

7
AUNTIE MAG

As Auntie Mag walked out that Monday morning, her face was full of defiance. She would walk like a champion no matter what the people said of her. She had known ridicule all her life. It had been hard to feel rejected and unwanted and now it was even more so. It was almost as though her whole life had been turned upside down. She had nothing to hope for, no future before her, just a life of squalid existence there in the bush taking care of goats. But deep down was the determination to forego all those feelings and to grow. Her human spirit was still strong bolstered by her religious belief in a God that cared for her. He had seen too much of the world and too much of her to abandon her to the mercy of the naysayers. She knew that she would be the subject of mockery but she was determined.

She needed to buy bread. There was little food in her house. As she walked she thought of how she would plant vegetables for sale and get a few more chickens to supply her with eggs. It was while she was just coming onto the main road that a familiar van drove up beside her and came to a halt. It was Put who came to distribute the famous St Bess hand buns and who also sold delicious peg breads to the people in the area. He came from South St Bess and had been a friend of Auntie Mag for years.

He looked out of the window of the van and hailed her.

"Wha happen Maggie? You all right?" he called to her.

"As can be expected." replied Maggie.

No man something wrong, thought Put, Mag always had a smile on her face.

Put sat in the van and waited a while. Then he said gently, he had always been fond of this strange woman.

"Talk to me. What happen now?"

"Put, you come from the Savannah, you know a woman name Ruby Myers?"

"Ruby? Who nuh know Ruby? Wildest woman in the Savannah. What happen? She trouble you?"

"No but she coming to live up here with Long Dan. Them getting married"

"Long Dan? The tax collector? I wonder if him know what him getting into. That woman throw way baby like dishwater."

Auntie Mag's ears perked up visibly. Now she was into news. Valuable news.

"What she look like?" she asked.

"Brown skinned. Long hair. Pretty, but bad as sore. Every man know her."

"Well them announce it in church say they getting married. Soon too. She coming to share Long Dan bed."

Auntie Mag was jubilant. She had news. News that was important. Long Dan was going to be punished for what she regarded as his crime. She smiled.

"Put, just sell me a hand bun and about a shilling worth of the peg bread You have me from going to the shop. God knows everything and I too tired to walk the distance. I have to get back home to the goats. Them is my only companion. Them nuh let me down ever. Them better than people."

Put wrapped the hand bun and the peg bread in brown paper and handed it to Auntie Mag. He said nothing else as he took the shilling and the nine pence and put it in the thread bag that hung at his side. He was going to the village square and he knew he would hear the whole story there. What a prekeh! Something gone wrong. Love affair no doubt. Poor Auntie Mag. If she would just fix up herself she would get a good man but living there in the bushes by herself with the goats not helping. Anyway, is so life go. Put put the van in gear and started off down the road. Auntie Mag stood for a while looking as the van rolled away down the corner. She had the ammunition thanks to Put and she would use it well. But how? She smiled to herself. Vengeance was hers. Long Dan probably would marry Ruby but she would spread the news about Ruby and she would give her hell. Mag put religion out the window as she contemplated her next move. She walked from the main road down the rugged pathway to her own home. Thanks to her parents she had a roof over her head and she had the goats and the chickens. She remembered her resolve to start a vegetable garden and get herself a few more chickens. As she walked she tried to think but it was difficult to come to some conclusion as to what to do next. She entered her compound and picked a lime from the lime tree. She would make limeade and have a slice of hand bun and two pegs of bread. She went to her kitchen that stood some distance from the house and did just that.

Later that evening she made up her mind. She was going to act cool as though Ruby was her friend. That was the best way to catch her unawares. First, she had to soft soap Long Dan and get back her job as the helper. She had to clean the church even better than before and behave like a sweet, kind, deeply reli-gious woman. That was how everyone would think that she had been tamed by circumstances. After that she would make her move even though she had no idea what her move would be. She would wait and see.

Auntie Mag ventured out that evening to put her goats in the pen. Saracen the ram goat was her favourite. She remembered the stories in the Bible about sacrifices being made and she decided to do something about Saracen. Saracen was worth a lot of money but her relationship with Long Dan was worth much more. She knelt down in front of Saracen who was chewing grass and looking at her blankly.

"Saracen" she addressed him, "I am asking you to do me a favour. I have been kind to you all your life. Now I am asking you to be kind to me. I am going to ask you to be curried goat on my behalf."

Saracen looked blank and continued chewing grass.

"Will you Saracen?" asked Auntie Mag. Saracen bent his head to pull more grass and Auntie Mag took that as a yes. "Good," she said.

Auntie Mag took in the goats and closed the pen. Tomorrow would take care of itself. She resolved to give Put something for his Christmas. He had made her job so much easier. She would get Long Dan yet. Yes, maybe there would have to be a divorce, maybe not, maybe she would work fast and no wedding would take place. But Saracen was willing and that was all she needed for the moment.

8

LONG DAN

Early Wednesday morning a little before day light shone on his house, Long Dan heard a familiar voice calling.

"MR Dan, Mr Dan,

Now who was calling me Mr Dan? Long Dan wondered. That was the address given to a gentleman not to someone like him? His name was Long Dan to some and Mass Dan to others. Long Dan pulled on his slippers and left the bed. The sun was also calling him he thought as he saw the first sliver of light peep through the night clouds.

He opened the door and blinked in sheer astonishment.

Auntie Mag and a huge ram goat stood in his front yard. It was a humble penitent woman who stood before him and Long Dan was full of pity. Poor old Mag he thought as he looked at her face in the growing light. She wore a red dress that looked new or almost new and she stood there looking contrite and alone.

"Mr Dan I giving you this ram goat for you wedding. Is all I have to give."

The ram goat looked about to rebel.

"But But I can't take that from you. I will pay you for it. How much you asking?"

"Me nuh know you hear Mass Dan. Anything you give me I will take it. I wish you well in your new married life. Me wondering if you will still employ me in spite of everything."

"But yes, Auntie Mag. I going to need you. Ruby can't manage everything what with a baby coming."

"But Mass Dan you work fast man. Baby? Me never know that start already."

"I kind of don't want it spread around yet. You understand? So keep that to yourself I tell you what the goat is a big goat What if I give you one pound for it?"

"One whole pound. I can't tell when me ever get so much money for a goat. But thanks, I will take it. God bless you so when me to come back to work?"

"How about tomorrow? The place need a good cleaning. I have to rush out I don't want to miss the bus to town"

"Alright tomorrow then . Take it easy Mass Dan and thanks. I will collect the money tomorrow. I will tie the goat at the back of the house. Only hope no dog no kill it but Saracen bigger than the dog them Alright. Mass Dan."

Long Dan hurriedly fixed breakfast and after looking once more at the goat at the back garden, he dressed and walked down the road to the village to catch the bus. He was puzzled but grateful that Auntie Mag seemed to have given up on him and changed from the anger that was in her that past Sunday morning. But at the same time her wondered how safe it was to leave Ruby and the baby alone with her. Was she mad really mad like those he had heard about or read about in the newspapers? He would have to be careful. A jealous woman could be dangerous and now she knew that a baby was on the way he had to warn Ruby but how? Ruby was likely to think that something had gone on between them. A woman living alone in the bush with no visitors and no people around, just goats and chickens was likely to go mad.

The bus arrived and Long Dan took his seat. He was really worried now but he could not say a word to anyone. Why had he accepted her offer? What was she likely to do? Or was the goat a peace offering that the good book spoke about so often? He hoped it was. The bus stopped about seven times along the way and when they reached the town, the sun was already climbing the sky. Long Dan walked rapidly down to his work place and entered the door way. The workers seemed to be late as he was and he was relieved that his lateness was not his alone, Before he started work however, he decided to write to Ruby so that she would get it in the mail before the weekend when he would go down to St Bess to tell her that they had to postpone the wedding by a month. It was a difficult letter to write when he had finished, he put it in an envelope and sealed it. He would post it at lunch time.

Meanwhile his desk was full of work and he settled to it with a vengeance. Maggie had to wait. He had better things to do with his time.

9
RUBY

When Ruby received the letter on the Friday, she was puzzled. Was something wrong? Dan rarely wrote to her as he usually came to visit. She hesitated, expecting bad news then rapidly tore the envelope open and read the missive. Some interfering woman she said to herself as she read the letter a second time. Dan wrote so well and his handwriting was so good, no wonder he had a job in the tax office. Then she squared her shoulders, read the letter a third time and smiled. "Well, that woman had better watch out. I coming for her." Ruby loved to fight. She had been fighting all her life and God help the ones who opposed her. She would fight tooth and nail for her man. He was hers plain and simple just hers as the wedding ring and the signed documents would prove later on. She was the woman Dan loved and that was that.

Nevertheless, she hardly slept that night. Did Dan have a mistress somewhere that he was hiding? She was not going to put up with a second woman in his life. It had to be only her, Ruby. She would reign supreme. Next morning Ruby knew he would come to her as he had said in the letter so she put on her newest maternity dress and fixed her hair. She wanted to remind him that she was carrying his child. At least she hoped it was his. She was still not sure.

When Dan arrived on the bus that Saturday morning he had a sombre look, a worried look.

"Dan, what wrong? What on you mind?" asked Ruby anxiously.

"Just something I wasn't aware of."

"Like what?"

"A woman in love with me even though I never encourage it or anything." Dan held down his head.

Ruby burst into laughter." Then you nuh shoulda proud. If so much woman love you it mean you are a catch. Dan, you tall, you handsome and you have a good job in an office. You made for marriage, but just remember, I not sharing you with anybody, right? You are mine from now on. When the ring on mi finger, is just me and you and the pickney in mi belly. You understand?"

"That's another thing. I need to put off the wedding by a month. And have a bigger one in the town Pastor say he will arrange for us to have it at the parish church and have the feed at the church house. You woulda like that? I want it to be something that we will all remember."

"Oh Dan that's why I love you so. I looking forward to me wedding day. We can send out good invitations and thing. I just hope that the wedding dress will fit. The baby growing you know."

"Yeah man I know. We soon have a little one to take care of."

Long Dan was livelier now. He had thought that Ruby would object and be suspicious. But she was not, she just jubilant that she would have a real wedding day in the town with a bigger crowd than before.

Ruby's mother called them to the large kitchen and they had

lunch. Ruby broke the news to her and she frowned. Long Dan looked on anxiously hoping that there would be no detailed questioning. But there wasn't. Ruby would deal with that later on after he had gone.

After eating they went back to the house to plan.. Then they began to think about food and what to serve. Dan told Ruby that he already had a goat and that they would need chickens and beef for the menu. Rice and peas and vegetables would make up the rest of the meal. They had to think of amounts as people would probably bring their children and other adults. In country weddings the whole district turned out and demanded to be fed even if there was no invitation coming their way. It was a chance for every one to put on their finery and eat and drink and be merry. Of course, there had to be rum and beer and a drink for the women and children. Ruby's mom would make the cake and there had be plenty of that too.

Dan began to look a bit worried as he thought that he would have to foot the bill. Ruby looked at him with a smile.

"Don't worry," she said "Daddy providing the chickens and a cow. You already have the goat. Is just the rice and the peas that you could provide. And Mama going to bake the cake as she good at that. Is my wedding too, you know."

Ruby and her mother found paper and pen and began to list the names of the guests. They knew that it hardly made any sense as the whole village and beyond would find their way to the town for the wedding. They knew too that they would get a bus as a charter and get a ride in. The people would get the best clothes and new shoes for the occasion and the children would be in crinolines and shoes and socks something they never wore to school as they went barefoot to everything in the village except to church. But the official invitations would have to be sent out to the important people in that section of St Bess, and in South Manchester to the school teachers, the local pastors the postmistress, the police men and the businessmen who held the money and who owned the shops.

Next they decided on who would be the bridesmaids and the flower girls and the page boy who would come with the ring. Of course the dressmakers had to be alerted as the clothes had to be made in time and Ruby and her mother had to provide the materials for the clothes of those who would be taking part in the procession.

Ruby grew more excited as she felt the baby move inside her as though even the baby approved of this move she was making. She was happy. It would be the wedding of the year and everyone would be green with envy she knew.

Ruby and her Mom had a lot of work to do now including getting the ingredients for the cake and the spices and every-thing else for the food . Everyone had to have a lot of food. They had to choose now who to be cooks and they were not to feel like servants but as important people and part of the whole occasion.

Also the bride had to have flowers and there had to be rose-buds for the flower girls and bridesmaids and the church had to be decorated beforehand. There were so many things to be done that the two women began to feel overwhelmed and Ruby's Mom began to wonder if it could be achieved in so short a time. Ruby's baby was growing inside her and the wedding had to take place before it began to show. Was it worth it they both began to wonder but they were so taken with the flow and the excitement and the show that such a wedding would be for the parishes and themselves that they silently agreed, yes it would be worth everything, the money, the effort, and all the fuss.

10
THE WEDDING

The parish of St Bess was agog with excitement all the way to the wedding day. So were those in the village in the neighbouring parish where Long Dan lived. Buses were hired to take the people into the local town and the church was full, so full that the pastor suggested getting a tent put up outside with benches from the school to accommodate those who had no seats inside the church building. Children were everywhere. Mothers sat and fanned themselves in the heat and men stood about in groups chatting and looking forward to the food and the festivities. Some hoped to get drunk and go home to sleep it off. Others hoped that the speeches would not be long and that the food would be good.

Auntie Mag was there and she hovered between the kitchen in the building close to the church house where the reception was to be held, and the church. She walked about in all her finery, head held up as proud as Saracen the ram goat used to be when he surveyed her as she put him in his pen. Now Saracen was in a huge pot with curry and other seasoning. She held her breath as she saw the pot bubbling and smelled the pungent curry in her nostrils. But there was a wicked smile on her face. She swore that Saracen was somewhere close by in spirit and saw what she did with that pot of curry. Saracen was her sacrifice to her own sorrows. Auntie Mag went back to the church and sat at the back in the pew closest to the door that the bride would come through up the steps. She wanted to see this bride who had done her out of her dream. She sat in silence while people walked up and down and little children refused to sit with their parents.

The groom and the best man sat waiting patiently. Pastor Granger sat on the platform and the organist was sitting waiting to play the tune that Auntie Mag had hummed in her head all these years. Here comes the bride.' Auntie Mag was not the bride. It hurt.

The bride was not late. She arrived with her entourage in a large black ford car and a few other smaller cars. There was a buzz of excitement as Ruby got out in her long white gown and her brides bouquet in her hand and her head in a crown of white silk roses. She was magnificent and she walked in like a queen. The bridesmaids had on gold and the flower girls wore a bright pink. The page boy was resplendent in a white suit and white shirt and navy blue bow tie.

"Here comes the bride," echoed across their heads as the huge pipe organ belted out the song. People rose and watched craning their necks to see the spectacle. For once everyone was silent as even the children sensed the importance of the moment. The bride marched up to the platform with her father and the groom came and stood beside her while the others in the entourage gathered around. Long Dan looked extra tall beside his future wife and he looked at her with pride. The organ ceased playing and the people sat down to view the proceedings. There was the noise of sitting then everyone was still. Pastor Granger stood in front and faced the audience. He had done his many times before but never one like this for one in his own congregation. He too was impressed.

Dan and Ruby , s did the others at the front as the people sat and waited. The ceremony continued until the pastor asked the congregation if any one objected to the marriage. There was dead silence as some of the people looked round to see if Auntie Mag was planning anything. Auntie Mag's face was as impassive as that of a mannequin. Pastor Granger paused a little longer and looked straight at her. Not a muscle moved. Then he continued. Relief flooded the faces of the people who knew the problem that Dan was having with her and an ignorant Ruby looked somewhat surprised at this part of the proceedings. She knew there as a woman but which woman? The ceremony continued. The vows were taken and the rings deposited on the waiting fingers. A song and a piece of music played added to the feeling of happiness in the church as the bride and groom went to sign the bridal register. When they returned they kissed much to the joy of the onlookers then the pastor said "I now pronounce you man and wife." A cheer went up and the bride and groom departed amidst a flurry of rice and cheers. The reception in the Church Hall awaited their return from taking photographs.

People scrambled out of their seats and onto the grass as they headed for the reception centre. It had been a good show. Now for the food and the speeches, and all of them hoped that the Master of ceremonies and the speakers would be full of humour and that they would get a belly full of laughter and of victuals to return home for the night. The children spilled onto the green lawns and played to their hearts content. Although it was getting cool, the matrons among them used their handkerchiefs to fan themelves. Men gathered in small groups to discuss all sorts of things as they looked at the bar that was opened on the grounds and then headed its way. No one remembered Auntie Mag. They were too busy enjoying themselves.

Auntie Mag was nowhere to be seen.

11

THE VILLAGERS

The wedding guests ate to their hearts content, guffawed noisily at the well known jokes of the MC, drank the wine and the ate the delicious cake which was full of prunes and wine and raisins and some were heard to say that this was the best wedding they had ever attended. In some corners old men and women hid their belches behind their hands and children asked for more. The bride sat like a queen still in the bridal gown and the groom spoke his speech with assurance and poise. 'My wife and I' was met with laughs and approval and it was well into the night that the party broke up and the villagers headed for the buses they had hired and those with cars repaired to their cars. Some children were soon fast asleep and had to be lifted onto the shoulders of half-drunk fathers. All thanked their happy stars that the next day was a Sunday and they could sleep till sun hot as of course church was out of the question. Some more diligent farmers remembered their animals and the need to put the goats in pasture from their pens, the pigs would have to be fed and the cows milked in the morning . And of course the chickens but the free roaming chickens could find food in the yards till they were fed with cracked corn and cassava trash. But after all this sort of thing only happened at Christmas and this was added to that time when everyone went wild with the celebration of the Birth of a Child. Soon the precincts of the church in the town was without a single bus and a single car and the bridal party had separated the new husband and wife off to some undisclosed place and all else to their homes.

It was dark in the bus that was on the way to the village where Dan and Auntie Mag lived in South Manchester.. The air was chilly and not everybody had a seat. Those who were standing were mainly young men eager to dance while the bus wound its way up the hill. The bus had no music so they started to sing. The young women who were seated sang along with them. The older people were silent but tapping the floor with their shoes. Everything was jolly till a child screamed.

"Mama mi belly a hurt me Mama help me, me want to go to toilet"

The mood changed when the child threw up on the bus floor. Then Mad Ants said loudly,

"Driver, beg you a stop . Others joined, at first mainly older people then everybody as the bus stopped and the people streamed out onto a banana plot. They were all having running bellies. The place was full of mosquitoes and dark as pitch. No one had a lighter and the driver himself had taken to the bush so he could not shine the bus lights on the area. Some children were crying and the older people moaned.

"Mi going to dead now"

"Lord have mercy on mi soul "

"Dear God help me"

"Is what they give we to eat?"

"Is poison them a try to poison we off?"

"Driver you better turn round and carry we to hospital we a go dead now. Jesu Father help us"

But the driver was too busy to hear. He was vomiting and passing his faeces in the bush as was everyone else.

It was a dispirited set of folks who limped home in a filthy bus in the early morning. They took to their beds. Some hovered close to the latrines. Others refused to drink or eat. Rumours soared like eagles.

Some older folk had heard of cholera outbreaks in the past and blamed the water they had washed the raw vegetables in. Others spoke of obeah still others spoke of the St Bess folk and their ways on the Savannah. Then the bread man Put came around on his van and said that the St Bess people were suffering too and that Long Dan and his bride had ended up in hospital that night.

It was Auntie Mag who saved the people in that district from any more suffering. Armed with her knowledge of bush medicine that she had learnt from her forebears she went from home to home bearing good tidings and came out with a smile on her face. The village survived. At least one child had to be admitted to the hospital. Auntie Mag was now known as a healer and called Nurse Maggie by the whole village. When Long Dan came out of hospital he called on her to thank her. He mentioned the fact that Ruby and the unborn child were safe and how glad he was she had done what she did.

Maggie smiled and nodded her head. Not one person asked how come she had not fallen ill herself.

Auntie Mag was queen of the whole village. She sat on the bed in her little house and planned her next move.

It emerged that she knew the ways of herbs as her great grandmother had been a famous herbal healer in St Bess and that her grandmother and mother had passed on the knowledge to Auntie Mag before she died. Auntie Mag, being a woman of the church had suppressed the knowledge as she had felt that such news would jeopardise her position in the church. But she was glad for it now. The people still visited balm men and women even though they attended church and there were those who went to the white medical doctors as well as balm men and women. For the first time in her life Auntie Mag felt important. She preened in the village and took to wearing a head tie. She quoted the Bible as she had studied Bible verses. She spent time in the deep bush gathering bushes and drying them. It seemed that Auntie Mag would reign supreme for a long time to come.

12

WHAT THE VILLAGERS SAID

A poison them was going poison off the whole a we.
Lord Jesus take the case and leave the pillow
A cholera water them boil the food in.
Long Dan bring trouble pon we
A nuh him a the woman him married to
St Bess want to kill off the whole a we and take the land
But a wonder a what cause it?
Is obeah the woman a do a nuh human being doing this. Is a spirit them get to do it
But I wonder if it catch Long Dan?
Him and him wife spend the night at hospital
What a night them have.
But me nuh hear say them people at St Bess have the same problem!
Running belly like bull calf on the loose
Running belly like hurricane.
Thank God for Auntie Mag A she save we life
And all the time we nuh know what she a do in the bush down there

She know bout the goat them and she know all the bush them round here. When me sick again is she me a go to.

She have the gift, the four eye gift. How she know what to do? Nuh must the spirit tell her

Me say when me see the poor little pickney them a vomit up the muck me say a dead them dead now.

For two day school shut down cause all the teacher them was at the wedding and three quarters of the children was there too.

It was a national emergency.

You can imagine if we did all have to go to hospital?

We would a have to sleep pon the floor. Them number bed nuh deh.

Me a tell you bout Auntie Mag man. Saviour divine is she call pon the Lord and him tell her what to do.

But me still a wonder is what cause it. It did taste all right an thing.

And it was plenty food. Is three dinner me get especially the curry goat. Man that did nice.

You eat too much. Is dat make you extra sick.

A only hope this hit the newspaper and make the whole island know bout Auntie Mag.

And give her praise. She deserve it.

Give God the glory, Is cause she serve him in the church. Clean the church floor an thing.

And even the pastor take the medicine and get better.

Well I hope it never happen again. Praise the Lord.

Pastor Granger had to go to the private hospital and spend the night.

And them place expensive.

Them say that curry nuh good. It nuh fe eat outside you yard.

That a rubbish everybody love curry goat. Is that we celebrate with.

Anyway what done is done. Me glad say everything back to normal.

And none a we nuh dead

Give thanks to the Almighty

And him loyal servant Auntie Mag

13
AFTERWARDS

The newly married couple spent the night in separate hospital beds attached each to a drip. It was a harrowing night but they emerged the next morning weakened but otherwise OK. The bride's family went back to their village in St Bess themselves sick and wondering what their daughter had got herself into and just what was the cause of all of this.

Mr Bird's huge jalopy of a car took the bride and groom home to the house on the hill accompanied with all the paraphernalia that the bride went back home to collect. The baby inside her was OK the doctors said and the parents sighed with relief. It was going to be all right after all.

This was Ruby's first look at the house they were going to live in and she was happy with it at first sight. There was land around the house on the hill and although Long Dan hardly spent time in the flowers garden it was fairly well kept. Ruby thought of the flowers she would introduce to the land in front of the house and the food plants she would plant. It was a beginning for her and for Long Dan. She looked forward to children in the second bedroom and even building another room on the house in case there were many others on the way in the future.

It was evening when Auntie Mag came along to help. She was all smiles. Long Dan introduced her as his long time helper and close friend and church sister and Ruby welcomed her warmly and said she hoped that she would wash and iron an clean for her especially now that she was in the family way. So Auntie Mag kept her job and praised Long Dan and Ruby for still keeping her in their employ. For the rest of the week there was peace over everything and everybody as Auntie Mag set to helping the couple to settle in. One night when Long Dan went out to the village square he heard the praises for Auntie Mag who all the villagers said had saved their lives with her herbal medicine the night of the wedding. It was the first time Long Dan learnt the Auntie Mag's great grandmother had been a balm woman in St Bess and that the family had a history of using herbs and helping others with herbs.

Soon Ruby was going to church with Long Dan and villager got to know her. All knew she was pregnant and people looked at her speculatively wanted how far gone she was and of course what kind of baby it would be. They thought of names to give the baby and what the baby would look like what with Ruby being fair skinned and Long Dan somewhat darker than her. As was the custom they wanted the baby to be Ruby's colour. It was the response to years of slavery that had still not emancipated the people in the village. People still thought black meant evil and Africa meant doom. But those same people now went to Auntie Mag for healing in case of sickness and avoided going to the local town to see the white doctors. Auntie Mag had truly made her mark and was not anymore regarded as a misfit and slightly mad person who lived in the bush.

One night in the weekend Ruby sat her husband down and

declared that it was time to plan. The family could not live on his salary alone. The size of the family was growing.

"You know Dan how about us getting some chickens and a few goats. Maybe two ewe goats and a ram. Make sure some kids will swell the herd. And how about a pig ? This could be a real farm you know." she said.

"The problem is getting someone to help. You will soon have a baby how will you manage? I come home so late and leave so early in the mornings!"

"Auntie Mag will help and I am sure one of the young men in the area would love a job.. Plus there is enough land to have a vegetable patch and some bananas."

"You know it sounds good. I have a little in the bank to make it happen. I will see if Mad Ants or Tall Blacks will take on a part time work . And how about a breadfruit tree or two. You know I always thought of this but never got to it. Too tired after a day at the office. Now I am really excited. You are going to make this a real home" answered Dan. "A house is not a home without a woman" he continued as he looked fondly at his wife. She jumped up and hugged him.

"Me nuh want to disappoint you. Me mean it. You have been so good to me and everything. Danny I just hope the baby alright after that wedding night. Me wonder though just what was the problem. The cook them never use any thing untoward. Me just can't understand it, everybody just sick so?"

"We just have to forget it. It came to pass as Pastor always say. Nobody never dead. "

"Thanks to Auntie Mag. What a gem she is and nobody did know that she was a healer woman like her great grandmother. Everybody have a gift. Thank you Lord," said Ruby thinking back on that dreadful night.

That night they hugged each other as they reflected on the past and thought about the future.

Long Dan contemplated buying another piece of land that he had seen that was on sale just to give Ruby more room to cultivate. He had to get a goat pen built and he had to buy the goats for Ruby. He wondered which young man in the area would be best to take of the animals and help on the farm. There were many labourers looking for work but he had to decide who was most trustworthy ,one who would respect Ruby and not hurt the child on the way. The couple slept at last in peace.

14

AND THE RUMOURS BEGIN

Nobody knows who first whispered the news. But in the small insular district a stranger had come and all the people in the district wanted to know about her. Who was this pretty girl from St Bess and how did Long Dan get to know her enough to actually marry her and get her to come to this place to live as his wife? The men were envious of Long Dan and the girls in the district were mad with anger. Why someone from outside when so many of them had long looked at Long Dan with such interest? Were the rumours lies or did they have a grain of truth in them. There is never smoke without fire the older people said but the stories stretched from the sublime to the ridiculous and the people sipped it like refreshing hot tea from the cocoa tea cup. The oil was sweet as it swam on the top of the tea cup. Here was news. In the countryside where the daily newspapers almost never reached and where the radio was a rarity and a luxury to the few who owned them, news flew like the valiant john crow over the hills and into the valleys. Whispers were loud behind old fingers and fingers pointed like signposts in one direction. Long Dan and Ruby. Them people deh.

Them say is five baby she throw way.

Them say she have whole heap a man and poor Long Dan nuh know if is fe him pickney

Them say is because she brown why the man them love her so

Them say she catch Long Dan with stew peas and rice

Them say she can 't wash clothes clean

Them say she only feed him gungu peas and bammy like down a savannah

Them say her mother is a renking obeah woman so you mustn't even try mess with her

Them say her father have plenty land and money is that why Long Dan choose her.

Them say she never see the inside of a church till the day she married

Them say the first divorce in the district soon come between them two

Them say the marriage can't last cause it start on false pretence

And the rumours held the district captive for weeks until Miss Agatha boy drown in a water tank and them say that is suicide, something that no one in the district had ever seen. So the closely knit neighbourhood took up another story and Long Dan and Ruby were alone with Auntie Mag serving them like a queen . And the village loved her dearly because didn't she serve in the church by keeping it clean and singing alto on the church choir and didn't she live a good clean life far away from ridicule?

And didn't she save them from certain death when and gave them the bush medicine on that fateful night after the wedding?

People began to come to Auntie Mag for advice and the patronage grew as she did help some with the bushes that she knew so much about that she had learnt from her mother before her and that her mother had learnt from her grandmother before her there in the parish of St Bess.

Auntie Mag preened with importance. She doubled her efforts in the church, cleaning it with a vengeance and screaming the songs on Sundays till other choir members had to beg her to tone down.

The farmers gave her sweet potatoes and yams, okra and callaloo and the butchers saved a bit of meat for her and some women gave her totos and pone. In other words Auntie Mag was never out of food and in addition she washed and ironed and cleaned for Ruby and Long Dan. She bought a young ram goat and another ewe. And she increased her chickens and sold more eggs than ever before. Auntie Mag was on the way up.

15
LONG DAN

Long Dan went to the village shop to buy bread and a pound of salted fish since Ruby was not feeling too well one Saturday night. They wanted to have ackee and salted fish the next morning for breakfast. Sunday morning breakfast was always popular and better than other mornings. He thought the furore about the bad food had faded away as did all problems in the district after every one was tired of it as old news. But he noticed the stares and the furtive eyes and amongst the young girls he saw the whispering and the giggles, hand over mouths as they stared and then looked away. The shop owner, Ms Owens, seemed reluctant to serve him and said not a word as she dropped his purchase on the shop counter and took the few shillings he passed to her without the usual greeting or word of thanks. He looked around and people kept their eyes averted. He wanted to ask what the problem was but could not. He was afraid. He needed a friend. He needed someone who would sit with him and talk with him but he seemed to be a stranger here in the district in which he was born and where he grew up. He thought that maybe he could seek out the pastor but then people did not share secrets like this with the pastor .He was too remote there in his castle away from the real thing, the people of the village.

As he walked home that Saturday night he was thinking hard. What was it? What had he done? Did they resent Ruby? But then since she came to the village a few weeks ago she had only gone to church twice and she had scarcely left the house except to buy items at the shop. He had preferred to buy most grocery items in the town and take them home on the bus. Was that the problem? He had stopped buying everything there? Then it occurred to him. Auntie Mag. She was coming to wash on Monday. She was a real help around the house and Ruby had asked him to pay her more and he had done just that. She would know what the problems were. He decided to say nothing to Ruby as she would only worry and he wanted her and the baby to be happy even though the child was not yet born. He hoped to catch Auntie Mag the Monday evening after coming home from work outside the house with the wash or on her way home and he would have a little chat just to see if there were any problems or it was really his imagination. He thought he was going insane while he walked home that Saturday night and he tossed and turned so much in his bed that Ruby hardly slept. His instincts told him there was something wrong and he did not know just what it was.

Sunday passed with him being confused. He was asked to read the lesson and he made mistakes. He walked home ashamed. Ruby cooked beef for dinner that Sunday and he ate but little . On Monday evening after coming home from work, he went inside and changed then waited until Auntie Mag was finished with the washing and walking home. He joined her on the road.

" Auntie, " he said. "You have worked for me a long time now and you know mi ways. What going wrong in the district? What they saying about me and Ruby?"

Auntie Mag stopped and looked at him. There was a glint in her eyes , a glint of triumph but Long Dan was too confused to see it.

"Them saying that you can't be sure is your baby she carrying. She was a wild woman in St Bess. Every man know her there. She wilder than mongoose."

"Ruby? But she never give me reason to believe that?"

"Well nuh so love go! You never know what to expect It is blinder than young puppy.'

"Ruby? Wild? Me know that she pretty and that the man them love brown skin woman. But wild? No sah. I can't believe that."

Auntie Mag smiled than she delivered her message. "You lucky she never throw it way. She throw way baby like dishwater. She must did really want to catch you. Me warning you, watch yourself even now that you hooked like fish outer water. Is a clever woman that"

Then as she looked at his crestfallen face, her voice softened. "You mustn't believe everything them say you hear Mass Dan, some of it a jealousy. Nuff woman did after you. Ruby pretty and she brown and nuff brown woman get call all sort a name. Me nuh believe everything them a say but you watch yourself and love the baby when it born, that is my advice to you."

Long Dan's face seemed almost as long as his legs. His legs too seemed longer than ever. He felt tired and lost. Suddenly he turned away from Auntie Mag and walked back towards his own gate. Auntie felt the urge to laugh. But she didn't. Instead she walked thoughtfully along the road to her own turn off to her lonely shack.

As Long Dan walked into the house, he saw Ruby setting dishes on the table. She was smiling at him. "Me cook you food you know. You sure you not hungry? Come on man eat and you can wash it down with some limeade and the dessert is some corn pone."

Long Dan smiled with relief. This was the Ruby he had married the one that he loved and who was carrying his child. No, not some other man's child but his. He put his fears out the window and sat at the table. He ate and was satisfied. Ruby sat too and ate the food she had prepared. Long Dan was happy again...well almost.

16

PASTOR GRANGER

Pastor Granger was not a man for news. He was distant when it came to village gossip. He liked to stand apart so when Miss Gatha got a drive in his car, sitting at the back as any subordinate should, he barely listened while she spoke all the way into the town.

"Poor Mass Dan," she began after a short interlude of peace when the silence had been welcome while he drove carefully on the bad roads, "Him married to the wrong woman. One would believe that he would find a nice woman from the area. Him go down to Savannah go take up with a harlot."

His ears pricked up at the word harlot.

"Harlot?" he asked "But she seems a nice young lady to me" he intoned

"Poor Mass Dan don't even know if is fe him baby she carrying. She was a wild woman down on the Savannah"

"How come? He couldn't have known this before he married her?" asked Pastor Granger

"Mass Dan is as innocent as a baby lamb. Them say she

catch him with stew peas and rice. Is a famous way that you know Pastor."

Pastor Granger made a face. He didn't want to hear about obeah or witch craft. He was sick of it.

"But anyway them say she throw way several babies already as the fathers them didn't want to own up that it is fe them"

"Throw them away?"

"Well abort them. She use some sorta weed and get rid of them before them get too big."

"But that is illegal isn't it?"

"No police going to arrest you for that Pastor. Women do it all the time when them don't want any more children and when the fathers them don't want to own them. "

Pastor Granger longed for silence. He knew about abortion. It happened too in Scotland but he hated it Why? What was the use of the practice? He would preach about it next Sunday. The people would say that him spreading gana on poor Mass Dan and his wife but he had to speak against it. As pastor of the church he felt it was his duty to enlighten these poor little darkies in this country.

"Is it such a common practice," he asked.

"Common enough. The woman them careless and the man them worse. A so life go we just accept it just so" said Miss Gatha from the back seat.

Silence reigned again. Pastor was busy planning his sermon for Sunday and Miss Gatha was tired of talking. They slipped into the little one street town and Miss Gatha said thanks and went her way. Pastor went to the shops and made purchases. He hurried back after collecting his children. Then even though it was not his day for preparing his sermon he did just that. It would energise the people on Sunday. He would preach fire and brimstone on this unchristian practice, on another Sunday he would preach against obeah, that terrible African thing came with the slaves. Now that he had something to focus on he would preach as he had never preached before. He was too soft with these people. Love one another was all well and good he believed in that maxim, but some women were killing babies before they were born and some people were practising witchcraft. It was unacceptable in a colony of his beloved Britain. He had to teach they darkies a thing or two. He was here to preach civilisation too after all.

When Pastor Granger took to the pulpit that Sunday, his very voice was changed from the mild mannered man into a man who preach it come and preach it go just like the preachers in the other save churches in the neighbourhood. Some women came out trembling other men came out with frowns on their faces.

"Is what?" they asked, 'what sweet Pastor? Is who get him so riled up?. Me never hear him so bad before?"

"Him get it bad fe true. Wonder if him helper put too much salt in him food?"

"Or him wife refuse him last night? Him must be frustrated. Or a gana him a try drop?"

"But a fe who?"

"Me nuh know sah!"

It was Miss Gatha who provided the clue. She made it known that she had spoken to Pastor about Long Dan's wife and just perhaps that was what the tirade was all about. Some people laughed. Others looked worried and that was the topic of conversation in the shops and the rum bars for the rest of that week. Pastor Granger dropping gana as the bishop did every Sunday in the save church down the road. Poor Long Dan heard the rumours as he had gone to Church that Sunday and had wondered what the fuss was about. Ruby had not gone as she had not been feeling well with the pregnancy. Auntie Mag had been happy but she hid it from him that Monday when she came to wash his and Ruby's clothes.

With a long face and drooping mouth she told him what people were saying. Long Dan was frightened at what would happen if Ruby heard the scandal that was developing around her so he begged Mag to keep it all to herself . Ruby hardly left the house now that the pregnancy was getting on and no one visited except Auntie Mag. So he hoped that the rumour would escape his wife. He vowed that he would defend her with his life for after all she was carrying his child.

17
RUBY

"Lord the bread done and I don't have any bammy. No yams or potatoes. And I need salt fish. I will have to go to the shop to buy. Auntie Mag not around to help me out. I have to go myself. Any way the walk will do me good. Long time I don't walk and I need to know the people in the district. So here goes. I will go all by myself and buy these items."

So it was that Ruby got dressed and started out. She walked slowly as the sun was getting hot and it was tiring to walk with the pregnancy and she had not had enough exercise for sometime. She left the vicinity of the house and walked up the marled road past the mango trees that hardly ever bore mangoes as the area was too cold, past the bamboo patch that grew over the road enveloping it in a canopy. The leaves cast a lay pattern on the sky and Ruby felt the child jump in her belly. She was incredibly happy. As she walked she thought of her move to come here to the parish of South Manchester and she knew she missed the smell of the thyme and scallion in her section of St Bess. But this was a good move. She was on her own and away from the over protective eyes of her parents. It was then that she saw the two

young men who had come to do odd jobs some time before.
They were Tall Blacks and Mad Ants. Dan had told them that he
had no jobs now but later on in the year he would like to employ
them. They were behind her and they slowed down when they
saw her ahead of them.

"Is Long Dan woman that?"

"Look so"

"Look like the baby soon come"

"I wonder a for who? You hear what them a talk? Them a say
she sleep all over the place to get that baby deh. I hope the baby
look like him. Or else!"

"Or else what?"

" IF not I hope him put her out."

"No sah. It nuh merit that. Him must rear the baby. Just like
him own."

" Them say she was like a mattress down in Savannah."

"And him never know that she was like that? Poor thing.
Long Dan take too long to find a woman. Whole heap a people
here did want him but him wouldn't look at them."

" And him go take up trash."

Tall Blacks and Mad Ants did not seem to care that Ruby
heard every word they said. She walked on as swiftly as she
could just to get out of the words and the spite that accompanied the words. But the damage was done. She wanted to run
but the belly was too big, to lie down and cry by the wayside but
that would be admitting defeat. She wanted to confront the men
but that would become a scandal and she who was accustomed
to scandals knew that Long Dan was a churchman and would
not like it one bit. So she walked soberly on trying not to shed
tears.

Did Long Dan know about this? Would he hate her if he
knew? Maybe she could talk to him. Ruby was remorseful and
confused. Dear God I was so happy just walking and this

happens to me. Why Lord Why? Why me? I know that I am not innocent but please use your powers to absolve me in this. Forgive me Lord for my transgressions.

Ruby walked the half mile to the village square and entered a shop. Everything fell silent as the stares seemed to penetrate her and condemn her. She stammered as she asked for her purchases. Then she paid and rushed out. She almost stumbled down the steps caught herself in time and walked up the path back to her home. How had the news got out about her? Who had told her story? She resolved never to tell Dan about her past. It was too muddied. Ruby burst into tears as she entered the door. It was too hard too much to bear on her own but she had to. She had to mask herself. She resolved to go to church on a regular basis and sit beside her husband as any submissive wife should. She hated the idea of submission as she was by nature a warrior. But this time she had to if she wished to get over all of this and be a model wife and mother. Ruby prepared the evening meal.

18

SUNDAY MORNING

That Sunday morning both children and adults came out in their finest clothes still a little scared of the fiery pits of hell but hopeful just the same as Pastor had been preaching hell and brimstone for some weeks now. It gave the most pious women in their well covered heads with the huge hats reason to scream and shout Praise the Lord, Halleluyah when the pastor's voice reached its highest pitch. It gave them a chance to wonder and look around to see which people had the guilty face because as everyone had suspected Pastor was dropping gana again. The once quiet church was now hot gospel and many people loved it. They loved the noise and the commotion as though God was deaf and needed the shout to awaken his ears and wake him from his slumber. No one slept during the sermon now and Auntie Mag was especially happy for this for hadn't David of the psalms say to sing and praise him mightily? No one had dropped to the ground yet to roll and relieve themselves of the many sins they had committed but that would come. Surely it would come. The church that Auntie Mag cleaned could not be defiled as she, Auntie Mag was innocent as a lamb and as spotless as the communion cloth that covered the emblems on Communion Sunday. She was covered with the blood and sinless.

Pastor walked with a jaunty walk as the procession of elders marched after him. He had hit the jackpot. Now he knew how to stir these people. The church was booming, the collection plate was better now and he had no more fear about the next school fee or the cost of petrol to take the children to their special school in the town. The church was full and he intended to keep it so. Then came the noisy choruses and the clapping and jigging and stamping of feet as the people geared up for the kill. Who was the Pastor going to curse now? Which sin had been committed during the past week? No one knew. The sermon would be listened to with great care.

The pastor mounted the pulpit looked down on the congregation and said.

In the name of the Father the Son and the Holy Ghost.

The sermon had begun

"How many times have you read in the Bible about the practice of witchcraft better known in this God forsaken country as obeah? How many times have you been to the balm yard and worshipped foreign gods? Hands up those here who have never been to a balm yard in their lives, never taken a native bush bath, never practised obeah for self advancement or for destruction of an enemy. Who here have never sung a sankey under the watchful eye of the revival man? Who here have never seen things happen during a wake after a death? Hands up all those who are innocent of all these charges!"

Feet shuffled under the seat before them, Mothers hid their eyes behind their hands and fathers looked rebellious . How dare he? Who was this man after all? All of them had taken bush baths and it was not witchcraft. It got them well.

"So that is how it is!" shouted pastor Granger " all of you

have done it and you come to my church all innocent and well meaning and you don't read your Bibles, all of you who can read and you take communion all who have been converted and baptised. You have pledged allegiance to the God of the Bible but you go back to the false gods of your ancestors and you practise what is evil in the sight of the God of the heavens the true God of the universe. How dare you? How dare you sit in these church pews Sunday after Sunday and listen to me preach and then behind my back attended balm women and men as though they know more that the truths of the Bible? "

There was thunder in the church that morning. There was anger everywhere. Little children listened wide eyed, mothers squirmed in their seats, fathers looked sullen and resentful. Young women twisted their handkerchiefs and young men listened with open mouths. What was happening here? Was this truly a church or a courthouse where the judge gave stiff sentences to those who practised obeah?

Pastor Granger continued, "I have heard say about women catching men with stew peas and rice. Something is put in the pot to hitch those poor men to the deceitful women for ever. What it is I don't know. We don't do those things in Scotland where I am from but I understand that it is done here. Ladies and gentlemen there is a hell and the fire is truly burning. Wait for it or convert now. God will forgive you if you leave those practices behind you. I am ending this sermon here and after collection I am going to ask all of you who want to , to repent and give your lives to the Saviour to come to the altar to ask for forgiveness. I will pray with you. Please accept the altar call. Amen."

Many women headed for the altar and Ruby was one of them. People looked askance at her because they all knew about the stew peas and rice story that was said about her.

But it was Auntie Mag who suffered the most. She was the

descendant of a big St Bess balm woman and she was gaining renown in the district as a woman who knew the herbs . She had been gaining converts and she it was who had healed the many people who had come down with diarrhoea and vomiting after the wedding. She did not go to the altar but headed out soon after the church ended. Pastor Granger was the talk of the district for weeks on end but the collection plate was no longer full as many were displeased and angry.

19
RUBY

When Ruby walked home with Long Dan that Sunday afternoon, she felt all puzzled and mixed up. Part of her as happy to have gone up to the altar and she knew that Long Dan was pleased even though he had said nothing, but Ruby was full of foreboding. Did Long Dan know what the people were saying about her? Auntie Mag had told her that a couple of Sundays ago Pastor had preached against the sin of abortion, why had his message changed so dramatically over the last few weeks? Why had the sermons seem to have gone from love of neighbour as Long Dan used to tell her that Pastor Granger used to preach, to hell and brimstone in tone? Was her arrival part of the reason? Ruby was worried. Long Dan walked with her in silence, his face facing forward never seeming to see her beside him. Did he know about the rumours? Had he heard about her past?

The crunch of the shoes on the marled road and the sounds of birds in the trees seemed like minor explosions against the silence that lay between them. In spite of the hot sun a chill overtook her and she shivered. Long Dan never even noticed as she pulled her blouse around her as though to keep out the cold.

She had not used the stew peas and rice to catch him and to pin him down in marriage. She knew men and what they wanted. Long Dan had looked at her and really wanted her and she had welcomed his attention. She knew this. In fact she had never served him that dish during the courtship. Long Dan knew this, so why the silence?

The baby stirred in her belly. Two months to go before the little baby arrived. That was what she needed to cement the ties between herself and her husband. Suddenly she did not care what people said. She had no wish to look backwards. She looked forward now to a future that lay before her like an uncut diamond to be shaped and made beautiful. They arrived at the house and Long Dan opened the door and they went in. There was no child to welcome them not even a dog or cat. Ruby resolved to get herself a dog.

Ruby prepared a meal of rice and peas and roast beef for them both and resolved to leave some for Auntie Mag if she came by. There as relative silence in the house and both of them felt uncomfortable with each other. Neither wanted a quarrel and really what was there to quarrel about? Rumours? The prayers at the end of the service? Ruby going up for the altar call?

The sermon? What was here for them to talk about? Conversations seemed to be getting more difficult each hour and now in the relative silence between them there hung a tension that was not there before. What was causing this? Long Dan made a noise as he pushed back his chair and stood up. He had eaten little. Ruby looked concerned but said nothing. He went to the bedroom and changed as he had not done so before. Back in the kitchen Ruby heard him move into the drawing room and out the door. Long Dan had gone for a walk.

Ruby washed the dishes and cleaned up the place. Then she put on a housedress the best one that she had and went to lie down. She did not cry. Ruby knew how to deal with men, but this one was difficult. She did not want to lose him. As she lay there in the bed she began to worry. Whose baby was she really carrying? Would the child look like Delroy or Long Dan . Her marriage was at stake. Would Long Dan accept a child that was definitely not his?

It was a long time before she slept and she did not wake up until Long Dan had come back smelling of beer and was in the bedroom preparing for bed. She sat up and looked at him.

"Where you went?" she asked tentatively

"Just down the road." he answered

"Long Dan what me do you?" asked Ruby

"Not a thing. Me just tired that's all."

"Come, get some sleep. You have to get up early tomorrow."

Silence again as Long Dan got into his pyjamas and slipped into the bed beside her. He turned his back to her as she made space for him. For the first time Ruby hated the baby inside of her, the hatred burned in her for half the night while her husband slept fitfully beside her.

This was a problem she resolved must be solved even if it meant going back to St Bess to seek help from a balm man that she knew. When she woke that morning the sun as already up and Long Dan had already gone to work so she had not been able to fix him the big breakfast that she had been planning. She would seek the help of the balm man.

20

BALM YARD

It was the flapping of the flags that made her know that her journey to this place was almost over. It had been a long tedious walk from the main road. It was indeed a hard walk along the marl road in a leather bottom pair of shoes with seven months of baby in your belly. She had come by bus to the small village located on the St Bess Savannah. In the distance not too far away was the sea. She could smell the salty air. She stood still for a moment to get her bearings and to think just what she was going to tell the balm man was the problem and what she wanted him to do. She stood confused. It had all been rumours nothing else and she knew that she had not heard all of it neither could she tell the source of the rumours. It seemed hopeless to go to him without solid knowledge of the problem and what act she wanted him to perform. Then she thought that he would use his board and tell her the problem maybe even tell her who the enemy was if there was one. She walked on more confidently now. It was Friday and the place was almost full. In one corner stood a table full of glasses of water, flowers and bread. To the west stood a small thatched hut where the balm man did his readings and gave out messages to the people who came to him. To the east was his home where he lived with his common law wife and six children. In the centre stood some benches hewn from wood and they were placed on firm packed soil swept clean every morning . It was clean though here and there chickens pecked and the people who lived here met a diffi-cult time keeping them from flying up and mingling with the things on the altar. In the distance behind all this, a pig rooted in salacious mud and even further back were goats eating the grass along the edge of the property. It was a scene she as accustomed to since her teenage years when her mother had often taken her there to ask the balm man what to do to stop her teenager from bringing disgrace on the family. Mr Walfall, better known as Brother Wally had simply said, "She will learn nuh worry. There is some life ahead for her just give her the chance that she needs." Ruby felt now that Long Dan was the chance that she needed and that the balm man had been uncannily correct. She wondered if he would remember her. She hoped he would.

As she walked unto the compound some of the men rose to give her a seat. The women smiled and greeted her although she did not know any of them. She realised that pregnancy some-times brought a smile on people's faces. She smiled and joined the waiting group.

"Brother Wally working?" she asked

"Yes man you soon get through nuh worry. You come from far?"

"Yes, you know up in the hills and me have to take the evening bus back home."

"We will let you through. We have to make sure that we treat you right when you like this. When the baby due?"

"Two months time."

"Yeah man. The baby alright though?"

"Yes you know. Is not that why me come. We have a little problem with the people them near where me live."

"Brother Wally will sort it out. Him know the work. Him good as gold."

People fell silent as the sun that had been shielded by a cloud came from the hiding place and came out in full force. It was usually hot on the savannah. A chicken came right up to the group and bent to litter the place with her poo.

"Move." said one woman.

" Shoo." said another but on the whole the group ignored the chicken and were busy with their thoughts. They too had chickens pecking away in their yards.

One by one the patrons went in and almost all came out grinning. Brother Wally had promised to help. They had a list of things to buy to assist in the process. It was oils and candles mostly that they had to buy at a special pharmacy.

When Ruby went in she had to adjust her eyes to the darkness. The only window was closed and the air was stuffy. The thatch was old and the floor was really dirt stamped down but it was swept clean. Brother Wally sat in the midst of the room facing the only door. He sat behind a table on which was a glass of water and a round chalk board. He had a piece of chalk in his hand. Beside the chalkboard was a box full of cash, mostly five and ten shilling notes. Wally charged heavily for his services. In front of the table was another chair on which the patrons sat.

Ruby stumbled as she entered and Wally jumped up and held her.

"Careful, " he said in a low voice, "Me nuh want you dead you know cause it woulda be you and the baby dead and that is disaster."

Ruby smiled as sat down.

"Well, what you want now? You come here already. The

spirit say that me see you over a problem years ago. You never come alone though . How is you mother?"

"We want a read up Brother Wally. Me want to see who spreading all them lies on me. Me want you to help me get rid of them people deh."

"Me nuh kill people if is that you want. Me is a balm man not an obeah man. All right. What is you name again?"

"Ruby, Bother Wally"

Brother Wally scribbled on the chalkboard and then broke into a babble of unknown tongues. Ruby was terrified. Wally looked at her then and smiled.

"It is nothing to fear." he said " I just talking to the Spirit to get the bearings. You come from St Bess but you don't live here any more. You come here from a distance. Married at last after years of misbehaviour. You past coming to haunt you and is not lies they telling! It is the truth.

You chief enemy in the district that you live in is a powerful woman. She high in the church and she jealous. She want you husband but she can't get him cause is you your husband want.

Nuh worry the baby is his. I see where you nuh quite know is for who. The Spirit say that after the baby born you must get baptised, join the choir cause you have a good voice and be a good faithful mother and wife.. You have it in you to be all of that. Nuh worry bout the rumours. Is a nine day wonder. Them soon forget especially after you become a church lady. Christen the baby early. It will need protection. And is a boy baby. Grow him good you hear me and you will have other children. You young and spruce and God want you to live so go on you ways. Just put a small fee in the box for me. Just be careful of the woman. She hurt you already and she will do it again. Alright?"

Ruby put a ten shilling note in the box and rose to say good-bye. She smiled but couldn't help wondering who the woman was and why she wanted Long Dan. Brother Wally was finished with her. She needed no oils or candles and the baby was her husband's child. She was happy with that news. But she left with a furrowed brow. "She hurt you already and she will do it again." Wally had said

Ruby walked to the main road and waited impatiently for the bus. The Treasure Girl bus lumbered along and came to a halt with a screech of brakes beside her. The conductor jumped down to help her climb the steps. Soon she was seated and on her way back home. She remembered that she had asked Auntie Mag to cook the evening meal for her as she would be visiting her mother in St Bess. Long Dan would have a good meal as he always spoke well of Auntie Mag's cooking. Ruby sat back and closed her eyes as the bus started to climb the hill amidst a cloud of dust.

21

AUNTIE MAG

Auntie stood in the clean kitchen and wondered where she had lost out. For years she had been the sole proprietor of this kitchen. Now the competition had simply stepped in and won. Auntie Mag stepped out the door and walked up to the clothes line. The line was full of the freshly washed clothes that she had done earlier that day. So that was all she had been and would be forever –washer woman and sometimes cook. Maybe she ought to leave this district and go elsewhere. May be overseas far away and begin a new life. But how? And what extraordinary skill did she have but washer woman and cook? Going overseas did not appeal to her. True there was money involved and she could make a living overseas and she could return to build a big house and clear the few acres and invest in some project right here. England was opening up now after the war but did she have the fare to go? And she had no friends who were going and could she find jobs there that would be worth leaving all this behind? Plus she had heard of the racism and the way blacks like herself were regarded in England. But the more she thought about it the more she considered the idea. It was tempting to say the least.

She returned to the kitchen and began to cook the meal. It was ackee and salted fish. It was also her favourite dish. As she prepared the ackee she thought of how she had nurtured the relationship with Long Dan thinking that being of service would bring her to him in a meaningful way but that was not always the way to woo a man she had discovered. He simply saw her as a good household helper and nothing more She put on the pot of water to boil on the coal stove to put the ackee in and then she picked the fish.

It was she who should be carrying that child. It was she who should feel the pain of child birth for Long Dan's child not this other woman. She pulled her handkerchief from her pocket to wipe the tears streaming down her face.

Then she made up her mind. She had to get away far away from this place or she would always be crying. She would sell out the goats to make up the fare but she would keep the land and the small house. She would go to England and she would find work in a hospital or restaurant as a cook. She would try to advance herself there maybe go to night school and learn some other skill. She was young, thirty four to be exact on her last birthday and she was tired now because all those years of waiting and hoping had taken its toll and now she knew she had to go somewhere, anywhere to get away.

When Ruby came home she greeted her with a straight face. She had already wiped away the tears. She was going to be strong. She had always been strong. Ruby shared out some of the food in an enamel container and handed it to Auntie Mag who took it and prepared herself to hit the road again. She took the small pay from Ruby and stuffed it in her bra. As she took it she thought to herself. Not too long from now I will be working five pounds a week so to hell with you and your pittance. It was with a heavy heart that Auntie Mag walked up the public road and down the track to her own house. She went inside and put down the enamel pan with the food and she changed and took in the goats from the pasture. She gave the chickens some corn and collected four eggs from the hamper that hung on a ledge from her kitchen wall. She had tomorrow's breakfast right there and her little collection of eggs was growing. She would sell it at the shop at the corner as soon as she had enough. She had to conserve and save whatever she could because the more she thought about it the more England looked like the solution to her problem. She sat at her table and ate the food with a spoon then she washed the dish and turned it over on the table. She went to the water tank and got some water in the bath pan. She took it to the latrine and took off her clothes and bathed herself. Then she donned her night clothes but before she slept she had her time with the Bible. She was reading James for the umpteenth time . The only other book she had in her house was The Pilgrim's Progress and that was the only other book she had read from cover to cover except of course the reading books at school. When she read the little section of the dangerous tongue she felt some guilt but hushed it with thought, serve her right, she took my man. She slipped into bed and prayed before she slept. Dear Lord tell me what to do. She fell fast asleep.

22

LONG DAN

When Long Dan arrived home from work he saw Ruby curled up in bed fast sleep. He did not wake her. Instead he found his evening meal under a mesh cover and ate it with relish. He sat at the table in front of the empty dish and contemplated his life and what the future might hold for him. Ruby's time was coming soon and she was alone many days. What if the baby decided to be born when she was alone? She could not be left alone at any time he concluded and he thought of Auntie Mag. There was a spare bedroom. Would she agree to live with them for a while, he would have to pay her more and maybe she could transfer her beloved animals on his land for the time being. Good. That was the solution. Auntie Mag was devoted to them both, he and Ruby and she would be pleased to be of extra help when they needed it. He would speak with her tomorrow when he returned from work. It was Friday the next day and she would have the weekend to think about it. Of course they would give her time off to clean the church and prepare the place for Sunday service but otherwise she would be nearby and she would live in a real home at last not that hovel

that was only fit for animals. Long Dan smiled. Poor Auntie Mag
. What was that explosion she had put on in church when she
had flung her hat at him? But that was behind them both now
and Ruby had never heard about it. He was glad of that as Ruby
would think all sorts of things.

Long Dan took a cold bath put on pyjamas and went to bed.
Only then did Ruby stir.

"Night' she said although the sun was just going down.

" You sleep good?" Long Dan asked her.

"Real good. The baby kicking like mad. Him going to play
cricket. You watch and see."

"Well since your time soon come I think of asking Auntie
Mag to move to the other bedroom till you get it over with and
the baby half grow. When you can manage I mean."

Ruby was silent for a while then she burst in to laughter. She
rolled on her side and propped her head on her hand and said as
she looked at his face. "You know say you good. You think of me
every time."

Next evening when Dan arrived home from work, Auntie
Mag had already left as she said she as not feeling very well.
Ruby wanted Dan to be the one to speak with her and Long Dan
went up the road and down the track past the bamboo grove
and into the compound where Auntie Mag had her house and
her goat pen and her coffee trees where her chickens roosted in
the nights. Auntie Mag was sitting on a wooden chair outside
the outside kitchen with the thatched roof and the bankras
hanging at the side where the chickens laid their eggs. It was
such a peaceful place and Long Dan wondered now how he
could persuade her to leave.

He walked up to her and she looked up in astonishment. It
was a rare occasion when anyone came to visit.

"Miss Ruby?" she said.

"No , she is fine I just needed to talk to you."

"Alright, go ahead"

"Ruby going to need someone in the house when I am away in the days and if the baby comes during the night she will need another woman to be with her till the midwife comes. She said you can sleep in the other bedroom."

"But... But what will happen to all this in the meantime?"

"I just wondering if you could get Tall Blacks and Mad Ants to stay here free and look after the animals for you. They looking a place to live and they can hardly pay the rent. I will pay you enough to make it worthwhile. Say maybe you stay six months to a year so that you can help when the baby born and Ruby all right."

"I was just thinking of selling the animals lock up the house and going off to England to find work, I thought there was nothing here for me anymore."

"England, Auntie Mag? They nuh like black people there and they treat them like dogs. We need you. The church need you so think about it."

"Alright Mass Dan I will let you know tomorrow. "

"Good. And don't let us down. You could even be the baby god mother"

Auntie Mag could scarcely hold back her smiles. So she had prayed and this was the answer. As Long Dan walked with his long legs up the track and onto the main dirt road, Auntie cried tears of Joy. It wouldn't be forever but to be so close to Long Dan. It was a dream she had never dreamed but it was like one come true. She rushed into the house and began to look at her clothes that hung on nails behind the door. She had a few church dresses and three more to wear like to town. She had to get another two or three made. She had to get a dressing gown and two new nightgowns. Oh Lord so much to do now so much to do. Yes she would sell a goat and fix her wardrobe. Yes and those two young men can come and live here she hoped forever.

23
TWO WOMEN

Auntie Mag was installed or rather installed herself in her new home in record time. The two young men were now in her home and happy to find a free house. They too had animals and they took them to be with Auntie's Mag's animals.

Auntie Mag made the effort to improve her wardrobe. She went to town and bought materials and gave them to the local dressmaker to make dresses for her. She got two nightgowns and a housedress and a dressing gown. She bought a pair of shoes at the Bata store. Now she was set.

Auntie Mag also installed herself as the cook and Ruby could relax in bed in the mornings and also during the evenings while Auntie cooked the meals. Auntie ate around the same table as her employers, Ruby saw to that. Unusual , yes ,as helpers always ate in the kitchen. Meals were delicious with an old fashioned taste that Long Dan loved. Ruby got a little jealous as he praised Mag for her cooking. But Ruby hid her feelings and said to herself that it was only for a time.. Auntie Mag was in her element. She was not working in a factory in cold England. She was where she belonged, near her home in the house of the man she loved

After a while the two women settled into a peaceful life together. Auntie Mag cooked and washed and ironed as she loved doing work for Long Dan. Ruby dusted and helped to clean the house even though it was difficult in her condition. Meanwhile the time of the birth of the child drew near. The midwife came sometimes to see that everything was going well with the pregnancy. She seemed satisfied. Ruby was a bit agitated wondering about the pain but more so about whose child it was. She remembered her mother saying that at birth, nature made the child resemble the father so as to prevent any problems for the mother.

Would the child look like Long Dan or would the baby resemble Delroy? What if the child looked like the latter? What would be the reaction of Long Dan? Of course he did not know of the liaison with that young man in her district neither did he know of her former wild days in the Savannah. Or did he know? People loved news and her marriage had been news not just here but also in her district and places around. Ruby's nerves were on edge. Then she remembered her visit to the balmman and what he had said. That was a consolation but was it really? Everyone knew that balmmen told people what they wanted to hear. Sometimes she went around with such a long face that Auntie Mag thought was worry about the birth pains that would be there for sure in a few weeks . She, Auntie Mag, had never experienced such things but she knew of the screams during that time. And she also knew of the overwhelming joy when the little one emerged. That was why people had babies, she often thought, then to watch the child grow and blossom into a teenager and then a young adult ready to take on the world .

When Auntie Mag thought of these things she would stand and look into space and a look full of wistful longing would come to her face and then she would sigh. Yes, she was getting old and Long Dan was so much in love with Ruby, not with her. Life was passing her by . She would rush to do something just to forget. No tears she would console herself, no tears Maggie just don't cry. You are still young. Pray. The days turned into weeks and two women got along as well as the could each going about their household chores and talking just sometimes to each other. There was hardly a tension however, just an acceptance of the way things were.

One day the two women met in the kitchen while Auntie Mag was cooking dinner and Ruby came in for a glass of drinking water. She was fast approaching the time giving birth and was very heavy in her stomach. She took the glass from the cupboard rinsed it and then proceeded to take the water from the clay water pot that was known to keep water cool. As she poured, the water she smiled at Auntie Mag.

"I glad you are here you know. I going to need you help soon. The baby soon come now"

"Wonder what kind of baby it is ," Auntie Mag mused as she cut the yellow yam to place it in the pot full of water on the stove.

"Wish I knew" said Ruby as she sipped the cool water "Hope is a boy though. Always think the first baby should be a boy."

Auntie Mag smiled "Me too. How many children you want? You young you know. I bet Long Dan want about five or six."

"I have no idea. Just never discussed it with him" Ruby replied she finished drinking and turned to Auntie Mag. "You wanted to have children? " she asked her

"Well it just never came my way. I will love this little one just like me own" answered Auntie Mag hiding a frown.

At that very moment Ruby said "Look the baby moving"

Auntie Mag looked and saw what looked like a hand or a

foot sticking out from Ruby's round huge belly. She reached out and touched it.

""Good Lord the baby," she shouted with joy." Is mine and yours this little one" she said. As her face was wreathed in smiles.

"Mine yours and Long Dan's" said Ruby as she too smiled. From that moment there was a bond between the two women. The child belonged to them both.

24
THE BIRTHING

It began as one of those hazy crazy days with the sun gambolling of the leaves of the coconut trees and the goling birds pecking at insects in the yard. Mad Ants was working there that day and Ruby as lying down saying that she was not feeling very well. Auntie Mag was washing clothes and everything was following the pattern of so many of the days that had passed so when Ruby screamed with pain and hollered "Mag call the midwife," everything else seemed to come to a stop. Mad Ants looked up from the grass he was weeding and even the birds lifted themselves from the turf and flew as far away as possible. Auntie Mag rushed inside and then out again.

"Mad Ants," she screamed," call the nurse the baby coming. Run run fast. I have to put on some water on the fire and get the towels and everything."

She bustled about like a mad woman herself and Ruby screamed again when the pain hit and Mad Ants dropped the hoe and ran his shirt flapping behind him in the wind.

The fire was hot and the water boiling when the midwife hurried up the road with Mad Ants following behind. The occasional screams continued as the labour pains seemed unbearable. The clean towels and sheets were set out on a rocking chair in Ruby's bedroom and Ruby twisted and turned when the pains came faster and faster. The midwife hushed her "Alright, alright. I know. I understand. Think of the baby when it comes"

But Ruby was not listening she was too busy screaming. Auntie Mag hung about the room awaiting orders from the midwife. To tell the truth Auntie Mag was terrified. She had heard of the birth pains but it was not as she believed it was and first time in many months she was glad that it was not she, Auntie Mag, who was on that bed.

The screams continued and the nurse soothed Ruby. Then it was time to push. Maggie looked on as the baby emerged head first.

"Push" the midwife coaxed gently and soon it was out. It was red and covered with blood. It was a boy and it screamed lustily when the midwife gave its buttocks a slap. Then it was time to clean up both child and mother. Ruby looked at her child and even then saw his face. Long Dan's child. Same mouth and nose. She sighed with relief as she went to sleep.

Auntie Mag and the midwife did all they could and placed the child in his crib that a carpenter in the district had made. Mad Ants came in to have a look.

"Splitting image of Mass Dan" he said.

"Nuh true? Look like him father. A real man like Mass Dan." said the midwife.

As Auntie Mag looked on she had to hide the sour feeling of hate that she felt then. Now Long Dan was lost to her forever. Here were the wife and the child and she would never ever be in that position. She left the room and went to cook the meal for the evening. Hers was a heavy heart as she wondered if she would ever be happy again.

25

LONG DAN COMES HOME

It had been a long day at work in the local town. Figures and more figures cooped up behind a desk and as he walked home after leaving the village square where the bus had left him, Long Dan brooded. His thoughts were on his new status. Husband and prospective father, a family man now. He felt slightly burdened in a way that he had never felt before. And then he thought of the rumours that had been flying like crows around the place. Was the baby his he wondered. He was sorry he had not confronted Ruby about it but he was a peaceful man. He let sleeping dogs lie. He was not accustomed to fuss and quarrels. Plus he loved Ruby even though he was not sure that she loved him too. But she had been good to him so far and she was the progressive type. There were all those plans that they had for the land and the prospect of buying another piece down the road.

Crunch went his leather bottom shoes down the road. No wonder people developed corns and bunions on their feet he thought as he went under the bamboo patch. The roads were bad and the shoes were tough. The marl was not too dry now and the road sides were not littered with dust. It had rained recently and no one spoke of drought for the time being. He left the bamboo grove and walked up the road towards his own gateway. What would he find? But he was so tired. It had been a very hard day at work.

There was Mad Ants leaning on the hoe. So he had been planting out the cabbage suckers. Good. As he went closer he saw that Mad Ants had a big smile on his face. Long Dan slowed almost to a stop.

"Hello Daddy," shouted Mad Ants.

Long Dan stopped in his tracks.

"Daddy?" he asked

Mad Ants laughed. "Go look at you son," he said.

"Son?" asked Long Dan.

"Yes Daddy" answered Mad Ants.

Long Dan broke into a run and took the few steps of his house and burst through the open door.

"Ruby," he said as he entered the room." You have a son. You give me a boy? How you do? You alright? Praise the Lord."

Ruby lay in bed with a smile on her face. The baby she had just finished breastfeeding lay asleep beside her. The midwife and Auntie Mag stood looking at the scene. Long Dan sat down on the side of the bed and stretched out his hands towards his wife.

"You sure you alright?" he asked again looking at her and then at the young child.

""Look at me I am as fit as a fiddle' answered Ruby laughing.

"The baby alright?" he asked turning to the midwife

"The baby alright. Him weigh eight pounds and he come out without a fuss" she said "What you going to name him?"

"Me nuh know Dan, you choose. Me want him name after you" said Ruby reflecting.

"Not Danville. No sah. What about Daniel Alexander?"

"Those are good Bible names. That baby going to be conqueror" the midwife nodded as she said this.

The baby stirred in his sleep. "See I tell you!" exclaimed the midwife

"When him wake up me can hold him?" asked Long Dan wistfully

"But see here then nuh must a fe you pickney. Is the splitting image of you," said Ruby

Long Dan bent to look at the child's face. He saw his mouth and nose in tiny versions of himself He smiled "I am a father at last ." He whispered, but they all heard it.

Ruby smiled then she turned to Auntie Mag who had been standing in a corner with her apron in her hands. "Auntie you can share out the dinner for me? Give nurse some and Dan here look tired. You will take care of that?"

"Yes Miss Ruby, I will share it out, " answered Auntie Mag. Her voice sounded strained. She walked rapidly from the room and entered the kitchen. She had cooked peas soup earlier in the day and it needed to be warmed. She groaned as she bent over the coal pot to light a fire and warm the soup. Using her apron she wiped tears of defiance from her eyes. It should have been me. It should have been me not the red gal from savannah lying there with Long Dan's child in her arms. Why wasn't it me? God why? Why you forsake me all the time?

It was then that she decided that she must have a child before she was too old. She had to, no matter what and she had to have Long Dan's child. But how?

Auntie Mag decided to pray about it and to ask her great grandmother how to achieve this feat.

26

AUNTIE MAG

While she stirred the pot of soup on the fire, Auntie Mag schemed. She wanted to hurt somebody and hurt her real bad. She contemplated spitting in the bowl of soup she was going to serve Ruby but decided against it. It was a nasty thing to do and would achieve nothing. She couldn't hurt the poor defenceless child. The more she schemed the more her Christian principles got in the way till she felt like screaming out loud. "Jesus leave me alone"

But Jesus would not leave her and she served the soup to the family and called Mad Ants to come and eat. Mad Ants came in and sat and had his food.

"Food good man," he said, "How the baby? What Mass Dan do when him see him?"

"Him happy'," answered Auntie Mag but her voice did not seem to show that happiness .

Mad Ants glanced at her but her face was impassive as she ate her soup. He wondered why she sounded like that. But he forgot all about it as he stood and took the bowl to wash it.

"I think I hauling off now," he said "Have to look after the animals them at your yard."

"How they doing?" asked Maggie

"Them alright. Two mother goat in kid and the big ram ready to sell."

"Good, keep me updated."

"Night Auntie Mag,"

'Alright. Sleep tight."

Mad Ants left the room.

Auntie Mag went to collect the other soup bowls. Ruby, the midwife and Dan had all eaten in the bedroom

"Soup good fe true Auntie Mag," said Long Dan as he handed her the empty bowl.

Her sour face relaxed a bit as she took the vessel. "Thanks Mas Dan, " she said.

"You better rest a bit you know Auntie. You work hard today. You look kinda tired," said Ruby.

"When I finish the washing up and clean out the Kitchen," answered Auntie Mag. Her voice was pleasant now.

"Lord I wish I could come help you." Ruby said smiling at her." She turned to Dan "She is a good woman you know Dan, Good as gold."

"Then you think I didn't know. That is why she work with me all these years.

Mag rushed from the room. Her face was flushed and would show the blush if she was of a fairer skin. Tears would flow if she remained in that room with the two lovebirds the child and the nurse. And flow the tears did in the kitchen. She had to keep the sound of the sobs down so they wouldn't hear her. It was late when the nurse left and the family turned in for the night. That night Auntie Mag consulted her great Grandmother and prayed that she would reply in a dream. Mag had mixed feelings by now. Should she hurt or nurture? She was just not sure.

27

THE FAMILY BONDS

Over the next two weeks, Auntie Mag was too busy to contemplate her next move. She was swept up into the family as though she had known Ruby and the baby all her life. Ruby treated her well and so did Long Dan. At nights she was lost in two worlds, the world of hate and revenge and the world of acceptance and caring. She grew to love the child and would often rush to see to his needs as soon as he cried. She washed the dirty terry cloth nappies and bathed him every day. She made sure he was never hungry getting Ruby to breast feed even when Ruby was longing to sleep. Sometimes she fixed him a bottle of milk and enjoyed feeding him kissing him each time as she lifted him out of the crib. It was a labour of love and this was Dan's child. It was on those times when she saw the child's face and torso so much like Long Dan's that she felt a twinge of longing and hate. This baby should have been hers.

One night three weeks after she had prayed to her great grandmother she saw her in a dream. Even though she had never known what she looked like as she had never seen a photograph of the woman who had died before she was born, she knew instinctively that this was her great grandmother Clara. She wore a light blue dress and a bandana kerchief tied her head. Long white-grey plaits framed her face sticking out from under the head tie.

"So you need help with it," her great grandmother said," I tell you what, go to your mother's grave one moonshine night and pray to her. She will tell you what to do."

And the old lady disappeared. Mag jumped up frightened. It was more of a vision than a passing dream and she knew that she must act on it. But at the same time she regretted consulting the dead. Her religion got in the way. She was torn between the two different places in her life, the balm yard and the church. She was torn too between two different feelings, the growing love for the child and the hatred that sometimes ripped her apart when she saw the family together and she felt alone, left out of the picture, desolate.

It took a day for her to decide. She wanted a child Long Dan's child preferably and she did not know how to go about it. She had no idea how to seduce a man and she knew she did not want to. Long Dan had to make the first move and he knew that he would never do that, he was old fashioned and deeply religious. After years of trying to appeal to him , his eyes went elsewhere and he would never defy the church. Mag consulted the Macdonald almanac to find out when was the next full moon. Every farmer in the district consulted the almanac for things like days to plant crops whether root crops or crops above ground and they swore by it.

Mag saw the date and now schemed how to get out of the house at midnight and walk to her mother's grave which was some distance from her shack in the bush. She knew that she would go no matter the difficulty, no matter the church discipline.

The next few days passed with a flurry of hard work. Long Dan came home at nights and she gave him his dinner. Ruby would ask her if his shirts were washed and ironed and they usually were. Auntie Mag bonded with the baby so much that Ruby, although relieved to have a devoted helper to her child, sometimes felt twinge of jealousy at the baby's reaction to Auntie Mag.

"The baby love you, you know Auntie" Ruby would often say as she watched Auntie Mag and Baby Daniel and Auntie Mag would smile and cuddle the child a little closer. It was then that she would long to have a baby at her breast and feel him pulling at her teats. It was then that her determination grew. She would have that child before she grew too old and it would be Dan's.

28

THE CHRISTENING

The baby prospered and the family was happy. Both Ruby and Long Dan grew more fond of Auntie Mag as the latter did so much for them both. She was like the baby's grandmother even though she was young herself. After two month since the baby's birth, Long Dan wanted the baby christened. Ruby journeyed to the town the capital of the parish and bought a lovely white material to make the christening gown and she engaged a dressmaker right there in the town to do the honours.

She collected the gown after two weeks of waiting and hurried home to try it on Baby Daniel. All was ready for the christening on Sunday, Pastor Granger had been notified and the elders and Auntie Mag had placed the bowl of water in its proper space on the Friday evening before and other people with babies had been notified to come.

When Auntie Mag heard that she was to be Godmother she could hardly believe her ears. She dressed in her best dress and she fussed over her hairdo and she put on her best pair of shoes. Together they all walked to the church which stood on a slight slope a little away from the road and in front of which sat dozens of tomb stones most of them old, and crumbly. The family sat in the front pew. Auntie Mag did not sit in her usual place on the choir which was on the platform in front of the congregation, instead she sat with the family on the front seat facing the platform and the pulpit.

The christening usually took place immediately after Sunday school as it was not easy for the mothers and fathers to keep the babies till the end of the service which was sometimes too long. There were a good number of babies that Sunday boys and girls all dressed in their finery.

Most mothers wore white dresses and fathers wore dark clothing, some in suits and others in shirt and tie. Some had not attended church in years but the christening of their children was an important event and they had responded to the call to come.

All were there, that is, the usual crowd that blessed the Sunday Morning pews and the pipe organ started its magnificent sound. The organist was an accomplished musician and he always played well on Sunday mornings. The scrapings of feet stopped as the people listened and responded. Pastor Granger stood in front of the platform waiting for the organist to finish the piece. When it ended, he spoke

"Today we welcome our new born children to our service and we will bless them to live always in the ways of our Lord. Will the parents and god parents of Vincent Longmore please step forward."

The couple and god parents came forward and the pastor blessed the child who whimpered a little. One by one the babies were blessed some crying as the water was sprinkled on them and some just remaining silent. One child remained asleep.

Soon it was Daniel's time and Ruby almost dropped him as he tried to get out of her arms. It was Auntie Mag who quietened him down but he screamed as the pastor held him and sprinkled the water.

"Daniel will be a strongminded man" commented Pastor Granger " He will have definite ideas about life"

The congregation tittered and Ruby whose face was red with embarrassment laughed and relaxed a bit. When the baby got quiet in Auntie Mag's arms, Ruby, though relieved felt chastened . It was as though her own baby had defied her As soon as the christening was over the two women left Long Dan at the church and walked home as baby Daniel fell asleep. The sun was hot and they had to walk slowly so as not to wake the child. Auntie Mag shielded him with an umbrella. Long Dan , as an elder, had things to do that Sunday.

Back home Auntie Mag cooked chicken which was a rarity, and rice and peas. Mad Ants had killed a rooster that morning and cleaned it. He and Tall Blacks were invited to come and partake in the feast.

And it was a good feast. When Long Dan came from church the family got together and Auntie Mag shared the food. The baby woke and Ruby had to breast feed him in the bedroom . Mad Ants and Tall Blacks lingered a little after the meal and discussed with Long Dan some matters about farming on his land. Long Dan was keen and so was Ruby and Long Dan told the two young men that he had bought the land down the road from Mass Rob and he wanted to know what best to put there. The afternoon stretched into evening and the animals at Auntie Mag's house had to be made secure for the night and so it was that the day of Daniel's first visit to church ended.

Auntie Mag went to bed in a glow of happiness until she remembered that the Macdonald's almanac had named the following weekend as full moon time and she would have to walk the distance in the midnight full moon to her mother's grave to get her help.

29
THE VISIT AND THE DREAM

Auntie Mag had never really shown interest in the spirit world especially as she had grown up in the church and held a good position amongst the members. But she wanted a child, Dan's child so badly that she wanted to try anything. Plus she would love a visit from her mother whom she had loved very much. She had to use the back door that opened from her room and she needed to be as silent as possible as she walked. She had chosen the Friday night to do the walk. She was glad that there was no dog to betray her as Dan did not like dogs very much..

Auntie Mag went to bed as usual but she had changed into black clothes such as she would wear to a funeral, she pulled the sheet over her and had to try hard to stay awake. Fridays were heavy days for Auntie Mag what with church work, the baby, cooking and other things so she was tired and began to dread the journey in the night and to a tomb? She shivered with fear. But she had to go through with it no matter what.

She got up at fifteen minutes to midnight opened the door and closed it behind her. She stood still and waited to see if anyone was awake and then walked swiftly down the hill tiptoeing till she arrived at the main road away from Dan's house. She stood and looked around. Nobody there, she was safe.

But she was afraid too, not of human beings but of the spirits who she had often heard walked during the moonshine nights. Up the slight incline and then down passed the bamboo grove Mag walked. It was a cool night she had not taken a sweater with her. In spite of the cool air she sweated as she walked. Why had she embarked on this journey? Which evil spirit had encouraged her? This was outside of all she had learnt at church. Was she that desperate? Yes, she told herself, she was. She was growing old and she wanted to be a mother

As she walked down into her own yard she was afraid that the dog would hear her but she saw him lift his head whimper and lay down again. Poor old thing she had had him for years . she wondered how long he would live.

Auntie Mag cut though the bush quietly until she reached the family plot where her parents were buried. She stood amongst the tombs and slowly moved towards her mother's tomb. Auntie Mag was trembling as she had no knowledge what to expect. Would the spirit rise and talk with her or would she fall in a trance right than and then and the spirit would inform her or would nothing happen there but she would receive her message in a dream . She hoped for the latter.

"Mama, please tell me how to have Dan's child. I can't let him know. But I need his child. Please tell me" she said. fear lacing every word. She whispered rather than spoke aloud and as she spoke she wondered at her request. It sounded stupid, how could she have his child without him knowing? Was she going insane? She heard no answer from the tomb that was overgrown with weeds. Tears pricked her eyelids and she turned to go. This time she walked slowly and she cried as she walked.

Maybe she should have gone to England as she had wanted to. She could still go. She started to plan. At Dan's she earned fifteen shillings a week and the work was hard. She had heard that she could earn five pounds a week in factories in England. But England was cold and she knew no one there and black people were not liked there, she had understood.

My God what have I done? Where do I turn now? Please help me. When she slowly opened the door to her room at Long Dan's house she could hardly see because of the tears. She stripped off the black clothes and stepped into her nightgown. She cried herself to sleep but she did not dream. She woke next morning and willed herself to prepare breakfast she was so tired..

Ruby saw her red eyes and asked. "What happened?"

"Look like I have the flu" answered Mag.

"You better take the day off " said Ruby, "Take some of the lime and rum and go to bed. The flu is catching."

And so it was that Auntie Mag got a day free of work but her heart was heavy. She took the lime juice and the rum dousing herself so that she could sleep. She went to bed and slept deeply waking up only to eat the food that Ruby prepared for her. While she ate she had a difficult time keeping her conscience free. Here is the woman who is feeding me and yet I am betraying her. She was Judas again .

The dream came two nights after Auntie Mag had walked to her mother's grave. The mother seemed to come out of a dark cold misty night and moved towards her. She wore a purple dress and a black head tie. Her face was grim and determined.

"So you want Long Dan's child but you don't want him to know," she said " I will help you but is not a nice thing you doing. Get rid of all that hate in you. Is not good to hate. I tell you what, see this bush? It will make him sleep deep for twenty four hours. If you can get him to take it on his food when him wife not there, then you can go into the room and have your way with him. He will never know what you do to him. You will find this bush in the woodland close to a mango tree. It grow under trees as it don't like so much sun. Take it and treat him with it. But I warning you. Is not a good thing this."

Her mother disappeared as into the cool mist and was gone. Mag woke with a jerk. She was terrified. A cold sweat washed over her as though she had been in a feverish state. She knew the bush and in spite of the warning she knew that she would do as her mother had told her to. She had joined the world of the occult and there seemed to be no turning back.

30
FULFILMENT

Auntie Mag was as patient as a cat about to pounce. The poor mouse though, did not have a clue. Ruby was sweeter than ever and Long Dan, though not as communicative as always seemed too stressed to see anything wrong. It took two months before the time came for Mag to attempt the fulfilment of her dream. She had to seduce a reluctant lover while he slept. She was terrified but determined.

Ruby was taking the baby to St Bess for a visit, she would spend three nights there over a weekend into the following week. Ruby left and Saturday came on like a slow run over rocky mountains. Mag would be at home and so too would Long Dan. She would cook for him and do the chores like washing and ironing and cleaning the house. There was all the opportunity in the world and she was excited.

Mag had crept into the woodland and found the bush some days before. She took as much as possible. She put it to dry knowing that bush was best used when dry and they also seemed to be more potent then. She hid the bush under her bed in a paper bag when she took it up from drying in the sun. She would often smiled mysteriously when she looked at Ruby or Dan.

"Why you smiling like that?" asked Ruby one day,

"Nothing Miss Ruby. I just happy with the baby and all."

"I know you love Daniel you know. You not seeing him for three nights though. How you going to manage?" asked Ruby

Mag just smiled all the more. Sure she would miss Daniel but maybe she would be gaining something of her own, a little child and best of all, Dan's child.

Ruby left on the Treasure Girl bus that weekend for St Bess to show her folk how the baby had grown, and Auntie Mag had everything prepared. She would boil the bush and put the water from it in the food The food, which was stew peas, was for famous to seducing men and then with the peas there was clean white rice to go with it.

She decided that the Saturday night was the best night. He would eat early on Saturday as usual and then go to sleep as he usually did at around six o clock or so. She would do the deed at about ten or eleven in the night when the bush had settled in and he was soundly asleep.

Mag boiled the bush and transferred the bush water to the pot with the peas. She was cooking on the coal stove in the kitchen which was a building outside the main house. Long Dan hardly came in to the kitchen as people said that only maama man go to kitchen, kitchen is woman business. So Mag cooked the red peas with the salt pork and tried to make sure that Dan would not taste the bush. She doused the stew with onion and scallion, garlic and thyme. She cooked the rice to be light and easy on the tongue. It was a masterpiece.. She of course had none of the stew. She simply got a piece of salted cod and cooked it for her own dinner. It took everything from her to boil the bush and cook the peas. It was as though she was going to kill the man she loved for so many years.

Of course she was afraid. She had never done this before but everything in life had a beginning and an end. This was a beginning for her . The thing that scared her was the fact that she did not know just how it would end. But one of her mottos was nothing tried nothing done. It this meant she would have Dan's child then it was worth a try. She probably would never have another chance like this one.

Long Dan ate every bit of the food and left her to go to bed. He was soon asleep with a sleep so deep that Auntie Mag became alarmed. She watched him keenly going in every hour of so to see if he was still alive. The clock said eleven o clock and Mag trembled with fear as she approached the room where Dan lay. He was sleeping on his back. Her actions were swift and meticulous even though she trembled while she carried out her deed.. She covered him and left with her heart beating so fast she wondered if he could hear it from her room.

She went to bed but could not sleep. It was only then that she realised the folly of what she had done. What if she really got pregnant? How would she tell anyone who the father was? What would the church members say? Would she keep this job with Ruby and Dan? How would she feed and bring up the child without the means of support? Her mother had been right . She had done something wrong. She hoped then that she was not pregnant, that life would continue as it was and what she had done would be wiped from God's record book. She crept back to the room where Dan was sleeping. He was still deep in the land of nod. Mag burst into tears. She felt as though he as in a coma because of her. She went back to her room and cried her tears into the pillow then miraculously, she slept. When she awoke Dan was still sleeping. She remembered her mother telling her that he would sleep for twenty four hours at least. He slept most of that Sunday and awoke at about four o clock in the evening.

" Oh boy, I slept like a log last night and almost all day

today," said Dan, " I wonder if it's because I ate too much? But my stomach feels OK. You went to church this morning?" he asked Mag.

"I didn't. I didn't sleep so well. I have prepared some food for you. It's callaloo and saltfish you always like that."

"Good. I will take that bath now and then eat."

Relieved and happy again Auntie Mag rushed to serve the meal.

31
THE RESULT

For two weeks Mag lived in fear. She feared the consequences of pregnancy and she feared the disappointment if it were otherwise. At nights she hugged herself with the memory but by morning she looked at Ruby fearing that she would find out what she had done. It was a time of mixed feelings and Mag who had lived a simple life full of religious maxims and beliefs had a hard time adjusting to the new reality. She feared her church brothers and sisters. She feared the pastor . She feared those rumour mongers in the district and most of all she feared her Creator. What she had done was grievously wrong and she longed to repent but at the same time, she wanted the child.

A month passed and her monthly period did not appear. She catch her big 'fraid in the second month when the period did not appear either and she had bad feelings in the mornings and threw up. It was morning sickness. She knew she was pregnant by then. She wanted to see the doctor in the local town and decided to take the bus and go in when she was free of the household chores. Ruby was looking at her suspiciously too, even though her stomach was still flat and she tried to hide the bad feelings from her. Abortion was out of the question, she had done too much to have this child.

The doctor confirmed it. Yes she was two months pregnant. The first thing Ruby asked when she told he she was pregnant was Who is the father? Auntie Mag hid her face and muttered, "Me nuh know mam."

"Dear God is so much of them you sleep with. And I thought you were a saint. You tell long Dan yet?

"No Mam . You will tell him for me mam?"

"One thing I know, him going to ask you to leave. You can't manage the work!"

Auntie Mag burst into tears.

"You going run me in mi sick state?"

"I am afraid so, yes."

"What me going to do? Me nuh have nuh more job. Jesus. Save me!"

"You shouda did think bout that when you were doing the act. "

It was then that Auntie Mag decided that she really hated Ruby. She knew Ruby's past and she now knew her to be a hypocrite. She wanted Ruby dead just then.

Long Dan was a bit more sympathetic.

"Were you gang raped?" he asked "and when did it happen. Do you know the men?" These were questions that Mag could not answer so she simply cried all the way through the interrogation.

Long Dan gave her four pounds and Mag packed her bags and went to her hovel in the valley.

She told Mad Ants and Tall Blacks that they could stay if they remained in the smaller room. Thee were three rooms in the house and an outside kitchen and a latrine further on down the valley. She told them she would be glad for their company was she was in the family way and had been dismissed from her job. They were glad to be allowed to be there still and happy to assist with the animals. There was a big ram that could be sold and she decided that the ten shillings from that and the four pounds that Long Dan had given her would help her through the months ahead. She would sell eggs and the vegetable garden that the two young men planted on her property would assist her and them as well.

Auntie Mag foresaw a grim seven months ahead of her and knew that when the baby came she was going to need help both with the birthing from the midwife and afterwards from the two young men. At night she cried sometimes especially as she saw nothing of Long Dan who avoided her like the plague. She heard from Tall Blacks that Ruby had engaged someone from her district in St Bess to come as her helper and Mag tried hard to hide her anger. She was dispensable . She had been dismissed just like that . It hurt.

She still had the job at the church and she hoped that it would be all right to continue doing that but she knew that she would have to stop when her pregnancy was advanced. She knew however that she faced some problems there as she would probably have to leave the choir and she might be forbidden to take communion.

What had she done? She often asked herself and she had to find someone to blame. It was Long Dan's fault for marrying someone else. It was Ruby's fault for taking away her man. She nursed these thoughts until her feelings turned to deeper hatred. She even blamed God for not stopping her and her dead mother for telling her what to do in a dream.

Then she remembered her desire to go to England to work and felt regret for not having done so. It was a truly bitter Auntie Mag who tried to sleep in her lonely bed at nights. Tall Blacks Mad Ants were her only comfort now and she considered their suggestion that she give bush baths to the people in the area as she had done in the past. The people loved that and would pay her a small fee. Plus she knew the bushes for medicines so why not invest in a little help to the people as doctors were expensive and the doctors worked all the way in the town. People would come to her in their numbers as they were no bush doctors in the area. And so it was that Auntie Mag became known as a healer much to the delight of the people in the surrounding districts and much to the anger of Pastor Granger and the elders in the church.

32
PASTOR GRANGER

Pastor Granger had heard the news from Miss Gatha one morning when he took his children to school in the town As usual she had begged a lift in and she chatted the whole way in to the town. Firstly, he heard about the pregnancy and how Auntie Mag did not know who the father was. Then he heard about the bush baths and the bush medicines. He felt anger burning within him as he made his way home and told his wife all about it.

"She can't stay in church , " said his wife firmly, "She has to go."

"She has been such a good worker. One of the pillars of the church." said her husband.

"Once she starts these bush baths, the next thing will be witchcraft and you know what that means , the reputation of the church will be in jeopardy. Read her out on Sunday if she comes to church. I will be there to support you."

And the decision was made there and then. Pastor contacted the elders who, as usual , were in agreement. Long Dan was saddened by it but he too was in agreement and the Pastor and elders decided that they would refuse to give her communion next Sunday which was communion Sunday and then the blow would fall as the pastor announced that she had to leave the church community and not return until she repented her evil ways and cleaned up her act.

Next Sunday morning the problem would be sorted out, or so the Pastor hoped and he climbed the little platform to begin the service with a heavy heart .

Church began with a hymn and a short prayer. Auntie Mag had her usual seat on the choir on the platform close to the pipe organ as the service continued all eyes were on her and the Pastor but Auntie Mag sang each hymn with gusto. She had always enjoyed church services and she was unaware of the glances in her direction. It was at the end of the service, just before the benediction that the Pastor made his move. The elder sat up waiting for the bombshell and among them, Long Dan sat in his accustomed pew. He was a bit fearful. How would Auntie Mag react? He remembered the episode with the hat, He was glad that Ruby had never been told about it. Ruby was not in church that morning, she was taking care of Daniel at home.

"Will Miss Maggie, better known as Auntie Mag please step forward."

Auntie Mag stood and walked trembling to the front of the platform. She faced the congregation and Pastor stood beside her, the elders rose and formed a line in front of her facing her their backs to the congregation.

"Miss Maggie you can no longer serve God in this church. You are pregnant without knowing who the father is, and in addition you have become an obeah woman. You have been giving bush baths to people and giving them bush medicines. Something that is forbidden in this church. The elders have agreed that you are to be read out of this church for your evil ways. Miss Maggie, leave now and do not return until you give up that lifestyle and repent of your sins. You are not welcome here. Leave!"

Elders moved away as a weeping Auntie Mag hurried down the aisle and out of the church. She looked neither left or right she went straight to the front of the building and then she turned and said.

"May the God I have worshipped all my life curse this church. I declare myself innocent"

Her voice was loud and strident, powerful in its rebuke of the pastor, the elders and the congregation. As she left the compound silence reigned for a full five minutes and fear struck as the Pastor gave the benediction and added a short prayer. It was a fearful and penitent group who ate Sunday dinner that afternoon.

33
WHAT THE VILLAGERS SAID

News spread everywhere in the district and beyond. Auntie Mag done for now. She all curse the church, something that had never happened anywhere near or far. Even to those who scarcely came to church, it was a sacred place. In the rum bar that Monday night men gathered to drink and their conversation ranged from the sublime to the ridiculous

God a come fe im world. You nuh see the woman that we did think was a saint tun evil pon we? A fe who baby she a carry in her belly?

Nobody nuh know. A mussi crab in deh or dog pickney.

Them thing deh happen you know, dog baby

And now that she fall she a give bush bath

She soon start read up with cards. Boy there was a time me did like the woman you know but she never even look pon me

Me tell you a save you get save she did a hide her bad way them under her sleeve.

Me hear say a Long Dan she did after.

Poor thing and Long dan never care bout her. And look pon the pretty woman that Long Dan go get. The pretty woman all give him a son.

Me want one a them bush bath but me 'fraid she go curse me like how she curse the church

Nuh worry bout that. People will still go to her. Remember say a she did save the whole a we when we did near dead from poison at the wedding?

Me a tell you she know the bush them. A dat ago save her People will always sick and them nuh believe inna doctor medicine.

And she nah hurt nobody with the bush medicine them . She a help them. Poor Auntie Mag. She did work so hard inna the church and is this it all come to.

But me still a wonder bout the belly deh. A what in there? A which man baby in there?

Boy we just have to wait till it born.

A what she a play though, the Virgin Mary?

A coulda never God baby, a mussi fe Lucifer.

Boy you a cuss the poor woman. A how she a go manage? Baby on the way an no body fe help her.

Mad Ants and Tall blacks say dem will try cause she good to them

Them two boy deh? Wonder if a fe them.

No sah them woulda own it. Them is good boy.

Mi wife say that she woulda like the job fe clean the church and thing

Yeh man after things so hard. Plenty woman woulda glad fe the pittance

And so the talk continued well into the night. The bar owner was too busy talking and listening to know that it was well past midnight . When he looked at the clock and saw the time he had to hurry the men from his establishment. Some would sleep on the roadside that night they were so drunk and he, thanks to the talk, had sold a good amount of rum. His apron front was full and he was pleased.

34
AUNTIE MAG

Auntie Mag went at what she defined as her new role with a vengeance. She took a trip into town and bought materials of red, blue and white and took them home to cut and be made into flags to surround her compound in the bush. She got the local dressmaker to make her a dress of the same colours and tied her head revival style. Next was the table. She filled glasses with water and found flowers to put in the vases that she displayed there. She decided that she would pull converts from the church and go back to the ways of her ancestors. As she did all this she kept saying to herself

"You think that me done? Me just a come."

She went into the bush and got medicinal shrubs which she boiled for medicines and bottled them for sale. People began to come to her in twos and threes at first and then more and more. Some were her old church members and when she saw them she would smile secretly while attending to their needs.

Sometimes she felt a pain in her belly bottom and she attributed it to the baby inside her womb. She did not go to a doctor all that time while her stomach got bigger with the child.

She as too busy with her new found role. She would feel the child move and she would remember the time when she saw the baby 's limb push out Ruby's belly and she smiled then. She felt triumphant as though she had conquered the enemy, all who went to church and had dealt her that blow she now hated .She often questioned God, why, why me Lord? But she still loved God and hoped that what she was doing did not in any way displease him.

Auntie Mag remembered the revival songs she had sung as a child with her mother and grandmother and she remembered the revival rituals she had often witnessed at meetings in the village square in St Bess when she had gone with her parents to visit her grandmother. She decided to have one of those meetings on a Sunday evening in the village square there in South Manchester.

She had found two devotees in Mad Ants and Tall Blacks who had not gone to church since they were little children and a few other young men and women in the district also joined her. Some regarded the church as a place of hypocrites and they saw what they regarded as racism on the part of the pastor as not fitting the term Christians. Others were fed up with the kinds of hymns sung in the church and they regarded them as old fashioned and boring. They wanted livelier music for after all they were young but they knew that Pastor Granger would never allow the choruses to be sung in that church.

Auntie Mag was seven months pregnant but determined that this service in the square was what she wanted to do. The belly pain was still there but she ignored it cursing the devil when the pain hit her hard in her lower tummy.

The Sunday she chose was the first in the month of May and preparations went into high gear from the Thursday evening. Those who were still in the church looked askance at the preparations on the Sunday afternoon and noted the drums and the cymbals with distaste. What would the Scottish pastor say? They knew he hated anything with African roots. What was that Jezebel doing disrupting the peace on a Sunday after Church?

The older men walked past with heads held high and the women lingered a bit but remembered that they had to cook the Sunday dinner for their families and walked away slowly wondering just what would happen next in their little world.

Evening seemed slow in coming to the new revivalists. They were eager to try out the drums and the cymbals and to sing the songs that Auntie Mag would lead them in. At about seven o clock the singing began and Auntie Mag, the old choir member held sway. The songs were catchy and as the singing grew robust in the otherwise still dark air, and some people came to catch a bit of the excitement. Such things were unusual in the district. Entertainment at the church was staid and the only other place were the penny concerts held at the school which were few and far between..

Some danced to the rhythm. Others clapped and rocked moving their feet as they did so. There was a riot of music that Sunday night. Many Sankey songs were sung with Auntie Mag's voice above everything as though she was a loud speaker. But her voice had been trained to reach a high pitch and the others joined in. It was a night air filled with sounds that were pleasing to the ear.

Then Auntie Mag began to preach. It was still now except for the sound of her voice and the cool night air that settled over everything. Auntie Mag, the avid church goer, knew her Bible and she quoted it time and time again and in the midst of the halelluyah's and the vibrant Praise the Lord's Auntie Mag held sway. She was the preacher and she was the change that many had longed for. She made converts that night. The revival service went on until the wee hours of the morning and people began to drift away as they remembered the Monday morning and work in the fields for most of them.

The young men packed up everything and then hoisted them on them shoulders and that meant the end of the night service. Auntie Mag and the two young men Tall Blacks and Mad Ants young headed to the yard in the bush. The bottle torch showed them the way in the dark.

Auntie Mag went in took off her clothes put on her night clothes and went to bed. The pain was excruciating. She could not sleep. She tossed and turned for the rest of the night. When she finally got up she touched her night clothes and found blood. She looked at the mattress and it was soaked.

"MAD Ants, Tall Blacks come here quick. Go call the nurse.It look like the baby borning. Go fast cut through the bush. One of you put on some water on he fire. The nurse going need it. Jesus help me please God. Run run.!"

Mad Ants took off like a bullet and Auntie Mag prayed and prayed while Tall Blacks found the fire stick under the ashes, in the kitchen outside, found bag of charcoal and lit the fire for the hot water. The nurse came just as the baby was pushing its head through. Auntie Mag was exhausted but as she lay back on the pillow after the ordeal she asked.

"The baby alright?" Then she heard her baby scream as the nurse gave it a slap. It was fine.

"A pretty little girl " said the nurse as she held up the child for Auntie Mag to see. It was the image of her grandmother. Relief flooded her being as she lay back to sleep. Nobody would know just who the father was. God was still good to her.

The nurse cleaned up and soon the baby was put in a bankra basket lined with sheets beside the low bed. Auntie Mag slept. The faithful nurse sat in a chair nodding her head. Mad Ants and Tall Blacks came in to have a look. The baby slept. Peace reigned over everything.

35
CHRISTINA

The new baby brought nothing but joy to the small household. The nurse came often and taught the new mother how to breastfeed and take care of the child. Christina was a beautiful baby. Mad Ants and Tall Blacks, now established members of the home, helped a great deal.

The midwife noticed too that Auntie Mag had just a few baby clothes and other important things so she set about getting them. She went to the mothers whose babies no longer needed them and gathered second hand clothes for Christina. She bought terry cloth and made nappies for the baby and she went to the town and ought a small blanket, baby soap and lotion. Auntie Mag thanked her from the bottom of her heart and declared that whenever the midwife needed a bush bath or bush medicine of any sort it would be free of cost. The midwife just commonly known as Nurse Simmons became Auntie's close friend and confidant. The baby, though born prematurely thrived with the attention and love that she received

Both Mad Ants and Tall Blacks came to look and hold the baby every evening after she was breast fed It was a though

Christina was their child. They watched as Mag bathed the child, they helped her with dirty nappies. They cleaned the house and helped her to wash her clothes all the while taking care of the goats and the chickens. There was a time of drought but as soon as the rains came, they planted corn and gungu peas and vegetables so much so that they decided that Auntie Mag needed more land. The two acres was just not enough. They went into the hinterland to an old coffee plantation and negotiated a lease of three acres. They would pay the lease when the crops came.

The once lonely house with a half crazy lady became a home.

The once crazy lady was crazy no more. She had what she had longed for, a child to feed and nurture and watch grow. The villagers too noticed the transformation and always asked Mag whenever she ventured out,

"Auntie Mag, how the baby?"

And the proud mother would launch into a long description of the little girl and her latest moves. After all most children in the district were the result of unmarried parents. Some understood the curse that Mag had uttered that fateful day while others decided that the Pastor was correct as Mag had been a faithful member of the church an seemed to have fallen badly. It was not long before the question came Who would christen the child?. The hung like unfinished business Because surely no Pastor would take on the task. Auntie Mag had been labelled obeah woman.

It was difficult to find money to go the village shop to buy food. Auntie Mag often went into her thread bag and would give a shilling or two and they would buy beef or salt fish or salted mackerel or herring at the village store. Of course people were curious about them but the two young men were just happy to have a home and one with a baby at that. Then they would cook rice or turn cornmeal and place the meat kind on top in each plate. That was the watchman.

Meanwhile, Auntie Mag breastfed the baby and gave some of the villagers a bush bath when they came. That would yield a sixpence or so. She missed cleaning the church and living in Long Dan's house but nothing was as beautiful as having a baby at her breast and two willing young men to help her. Christina was the centre of their lives.

36
THE CHRISTENING OR NOT?

The question remained who would do it? But Auntie Mag was determined, her old church was the place. She had never been to a save church and she had served her old church for so long how could Pastor Granger refuse her? So she inquired of the villagers who had babies when their children would be christened

It would happen on the second Sunday of the coming month they said looking at her speculatively Why she want to know?

Auntie Mag prepared with a vengeance. Nurse Simmons got a gown for the baby and the two young men got white shirts to wear, Mag Aunts would be the Godfather and Nurse Simmons the God mother. Auntie Mag put up a chicken in a special coop to kill. They would feast on chicken , a really rare treat and rice and gungu peas sweet potatoes and sweet cassava. After the christening. The concrete floor was newly polished and the grass in the yard was cut. The baby would be christened in fine style.

As time went on, Auntie Mag grew more nervous. After all she had cursed the church. What would Pastor Granger say? He did preach about forgiveness. Would that be the result here?

After all getting pregnant out of wedlock and giving bush baths was all she had done. Had God forgiven her? What lay ahead? Auntie Mag prayed every night.

It was like a bolt from the blue that the Sunday morning arrived. Early morning before the sun drove wickedly from the sky, The three adults woke from their slumber. The chicken was killed and prepared, The rice and peas and other food was cooked and Auntie Mag put everything in a shut pan and hung it from her ceiling in her bedroom. No hungry thief would find it there. Then they got dressed, and Christina in her gown and they took the sleeping child up the road to meet Nurse Simmons on the corner. The walked the dusty road with the rock stone burning their feet as the hard shoes hit the stones. The Church. The Christening would come first as the mothers had to take the babies home. Then the service for those who remained.

Auntie Mag marched to the front bench and the others joined her There were four other babies to be christened. The congregation was disturbed as they saw the little party join the other families to wait.

That would happen next? They waited. The elders marched up the aisle with the pastor leading.. The people stood. Pastor Granger mounted the stairs and looked down. It was then that he saw Auntie Mag and her child. He frowned then his voice broke the silence that had fell as the congregants sat perturbed. There was anger in the thunder that hit the roof like a bomb.

"Maggie how dare you sit in this sacred place with your devil's child. Get up and leave now!"

Maggie stood with the rest of her little group as the little Christina burst in to a scream followed by all the other babies. They were frightened. So was the congregation as they sent up howls of protest. This was a baby an innocent child .The small group marched down the aisle, unto the steps and out from the compound. Then onto the road and they took the way home.

Nurse Simons broke into tears. She was a member of the save church down the road and she had never seen anything like this. Auntie Mag did not cry. There were no tears only anger and defiance.. It was still her God after all and he had never let her down.

37
AUNTIE MAG

Auntie Marched into her house and sat on the bed. Christina was fussing a bit so she breast fed her. Nurse stopped crying when she saw how calm Auntie Mag was. Mad Ants reached up from a chair and took down the shut pan. Tall Blacks found basins and together they shared the food. They all ate with spoons. Auntie Mag remained silent and soon the baby was asleep. The nurse took the child and put her in the basket by the bed It was then that Auntie Mag spoke.

"Pastor Granger is making me a preacher. I will start my own church right here on this compound and I will once again have revival meetings once a month in the square . I will christen my daughter myself. You watch and see.."

Nurse Simmons watched in amazement. The two young men started to clap before they remembered that Christina was asleep.

" Come outside," said Mad Ants to the little group." We have to plan. Nurse you going to be a part of this?"

" I am right behind you. We have to get a tent and benches. We will help with all that."

"I telling you fe mi Jesus never let me down. Is a beginning. Not an end. Nurse mi never work obeah fe kill people . Mi give bush bath and prayers. Mi know the healing bushes and when me can't find out the problem me send them to the doctor for cure. But to chastise mi daughter for that. It hard. But God is in charge. To Him be the Glory,\

The work began in earnest. Nurse, who had connections, contacted the Red Cross for an old tent. The two men scouted the area for old stools and broken chairs and even broken benches from the schools which had discarded them and they fixed them. Soon the new church was almost up and running. People in the district who had got help from Auntie Mag and were angry at her treatment by the pastor, jumped in to help.

The news spread. Auntie Mag turn preacher. Some were sceptical, others were happy

" Is full time one we own lead we to God. Auntie Mag is a good woman, Is she save we life at Long Dan wedding."

"Is here she born and grow. Her mother and father bury right here in the bush She is one a we own"

"Auntie Mag is a fighter. Is an innocent baby him disrespect. Him no have no right."

And so the talk continued Pastor Granger was the last to hear about it. Once again it was Gatha who broke the news .

"It look like you going have competition Pastor " she said "Auntie Mag going start her own church"

"Church? " questioned the Pastor, "She is not trained and who she worshipping ? Lucifer?"

"Come on Pastor Granger, she is a woman of God!" said Gatha

"A woman of God! Jezebel ! that woman". shouted the Pastor as he almost crashed the car.

Gatha, afraid of a crash, kept quiet after that and they drove silently into town. Pastor was collecting his children from school and Gatha was buying a few items. So they parted.

38
PASTOR GRANGER

Pastor Granger collected his children, barely greeted them and headed home. He was furious. The three penny pieces and sixpences would be fewer than ever. He resented competition and certainly not from a half crazy woman like Auntie Mag. He always knew she was half mad. After all he represented the great mother country. His other colleagues here and abroad would certainly mock him if they heard. It was bad enough to have the save church down the road screaming on top of their voices when he drove past them. They were uneducated fools, But Auntie Mag who used to clean the church and wash the surplices for him? To now challenge him? It was unheard of.. What to do Lord, What to do? He decided to consult Long Dan. He was educated enough to tell him what to do . He barely spoke to his wife who hardly left the house anyway she was busy with the sweaty tired children

He drove out of the manse premises and up the road to Long Dan's house. Left the car and walked to the front door. Ruby answered the knock and looked in astonishment at the angry man who stood there,

"Pastor, Long Dan not in yet," she said nervously .

"Tell him I want to see him." he shouted as he turned, walked back to the car and drove away at top speed.

He headed to the manse once more a bit cooler now in temperament.

"The Jezebel starting her own church," he muttered as he started towards his study. He was going to write a devil of a sermon and he was going to preach hell and powder house Sunday morning.

And he did preach hell to all who left his church and went to an obeah woman for salvation that following Sunday. Long Dan came in late the Friday evening before and solemnly told him the news that he, Long Dan, had heard. The tent, the chairs and benches, the pulpit made out of tamarind wood and the hope of many people in the area. It did not calm him down, it infuriated him further. His poor timid little wife started again to tell him what she had been telling him for years.

"We have to leave this bush and get back to Scotland. We have the children to think about. They cannot even play with the children around here. They will learn their language. We have to leave Stephen!" her voice became a wail.

His voice became louder and she was silent . She was the perfect preacher's wife submissive and obedient. The children looked on in fear. They had never seen their father like this.

Meanwhile the villagers spoke, sometimes in whispers as they feared Backra massa an sometimes out loud.

Is what wrong with Pastor? What Auntie Mag do?

Auntie Mag preach Jesus and give bush bath. What wrong with that?

Nuh fe we country this? Nuh ?we build it up?

Pastor preach hell and damnation cause we black. You think him coulda go with that message to the parish church?

A de suh hell woulda break loose.

The talk continued much of tit repeated by Gatha who was Pastor Granger's staunch confidant.

Three weeks after the famous sermon Pastor Granger went to collect his sons at school.

He sat in the car outside the school and waited. They always came running to meet him. This time the younger son came looking sad and afraid.

"What happen ?" he asked the child.

" Georgie in the hospital. He fell and cut his head"

"Oh my God!"

The Principal came out next. " He had a fit and he fell . We rushed him to the private ward. But he is conscious." she added "The doctor wants to keep him tonight to see what more he can do."

The pastor drove at high speed to the hospital, got out of the car and walked, his knees feeling as though they were going to give way under him. The nurse met him at the door to the lobby.

"You Mr Granger," she asked

"Yes. How is he?"

"He had another fit. It looks like epilepsy. The doctor wants to be sure." said the nurse

The doctor assured him that they would do all they could and as he went him that evening he thought of Jesus curing the man's son of that disease. How would he tell his wife? She met him at the door as he was unusually late.

"Where is Georgie?" she asked.

"In the hospital . He had a fit. He cut his head"

"That woman that Jezebel!. Stephen we have to get out of this place this evil island," she cried as tears came down her face.

Pastor Granger sank into an arm chair with his head in his hands.

"Yes. We have to get out before that woman kills the whole lot of us."

And so it was that Pastor Granger applied for transfer back to Scotland and was gone in three months, his jubilant wife and his two young sons with him.

As they sat together on the cabin of the boat home. He thought of the time he had spent in that beautiful country. The landscape, the beaches, the picturesque villages... and he turned and said to his wife

"It is a beautiful land and I had wanted to civilise the people but I couldn't."

39
CHRISTINA

Christina grew robust and strong living off the fruit of the land and the love of her mother, Tall Blacks and Mad Ants. With Auntie Mag's permission, they both built two room houses with Spanish wall and covered them with zinc sheets. They wanted to bring in their girl friends and start families of their own. Three were quarrels but they were few and as Auntie Mag grew in her relationship with the people who attended her church and the God they all worshipped and loved, peace, for the most part, reigned.

This was Christina world, a microcosm of the society around her. As she grew, she ventured but a few times into the village with an adult. The town was a mystery to her. She did long. at times to see the wilder world but three was fruit on the trees at every season there was milk from the goats almost every day, there were vegetables in the gardens and The two men planted yam and sweet potatoes, coco and bananas, avocado trees and peas. Some of which they sold with the eggs from the many chickens and as always there was cassava from which bammies were made every day so there was little need for bread and bullas from the shop to supplement the diet. Food wise, the only time of lack was during the time of drought which some rimes blighted the land and caused despair.

Auntie Mag taught her daughter to read the only books she had grown up with, the Pilgrims Progress and the Bible. Later, she ventured into the only bookstore in the nearby town and bought a reading book that they used in the schools and from the local shop, she bought a slate and slate pencils.

Christina was eager to learn and even at the age of five she often begged her mother teach her more " More, Mama more" she would say, when the days lesson came to an end. So she took to drawing on the slate, landscapes and animals and people. Formal school for her would begin at age seven and she would attend the elementary school near the village square.

Meanwhile she took part in the in the church activities, endearing herself the rest of t he members of the church community. The community grew and the church prospered. Auntie Mag was queen of the village and Christina was a little princess. While the men beat the drums, Christina would accompany them with tambourine or she would dance and clap to the rhythm of the pulsating music and the people loved it.

Iy wasn't long before Christina asked the question that Auntie Mag dreaded.

"Mama who is my Daddy?"

But her Mama was ready for that. "Your Daddy died before you were born"

"What was hIs name?"

"His name was George Milton and he did not live near here. He was a carpenter"

"Did he look like me?"

"You look just like your Daddy."

Satisfied with that answer, the child asked no more questions and her Mama was relieved.

At age seven Christina was to go to school. Her mam got materials to make her uniforms navy blue tunic and white blouse. She bought her reading book and a new slate and slate pencils. Like all the other students in the school, she would go barefoot. Her only pair of shoes were for church. She was happy and excited.

Monday morning and new clothes new day new life lay ahead for the little seven year old. She worried but was looking forward to a new friends. Hers was a sheltered life, Christina had scarcely ventured outside of her mother's compound and part from the people who lived the yard and those who came for bush baths and religious services she knew few children her own age.

Holing her mother's hand hey both walked up the road to the school. There were children everywhere. Auntie Mag took her inside the office for registration.

"How you doing Auntie Mag? How is your little daughter?" the secretary asked she had been to Auntie Mag for bush baths in the past .and she knew her well.

"She is fine just a little nervous," answered Auntie Mag.

"Christina will go to A class" she said and directed them to the classroom just as the bell rang.

The children were seated as Christina stepped in. A little boy shouted "Devil pickney" and the rest of the class took up the refrain "Devil pickney".

Christina was puzzled. Devil pickney? Why and who was devil pickney what did it mean?

Auntie Mag stood tall and firm. She said nothing Terrified at her imposing stance the classroom went silent except for the teacher who took the child an pointed her to a bench that was empty.

"What's your name?" asked the teacher.

"Christina maam."

"You will welcome Christina to our class alright?"

The students answered. They were afraid. "Yes Maam."

The disturbed mother left the child who was trembling with fear. She knew that Christina would have to fight this battle and she knew that she would win. She was strong.

That day Christina fought back tears. She was not going to let them see her cry. She wondered at the simplicity of the lessons that she was taught that day. ABCD the alphabet. The simple words that she already knew that she had learnt years before. The teacher for the most part taught the whole class paying attention to no one child in particular. Fearful to approach her Christina kept quiet just looking around in wonderment at her new surroundings as though wondering how could she endure this for so long until she was fifteen years old and ready to leave school. During lunchtime, she paid her penny and collected her lunch which was rice and beef, That evening she went back home as class was dismissed and went to the room she shared with Auntie Mag.

"Mama, what did I do? The children don't want to talk to me they say I am devil pickney.

"Don't you worry," her mama told her, "children will say anything. You just show them that you can read better than they can." But that night she held her daughter close as she lay awake.

It was the next day that the children saw that she could read even the Bible. The A class teacher, Miss Grant began asking questions pertaining to the lesson she had taught the day before.

Miss Grant saw that from her lonely bench Christina knew the alphabet and to Miss Grant astonishment could read the entire reading book and even the King James version of the Bible. The other children looked at her some with envy as she was promoted to the third grade and apparently could do well there too. It was there that she met a boy who would be her mentor and who from them mounted a defence against all who called her devil pickney. It was Daniel, Long Dan's oldest child. From that day Daniel seemed to want to hold her hand and help her through all the difficulties. She was now able to play with the other children and her voice rang out with glee as they played ring games and kept dolly house, hide and seek and even chase with he boys. Without Daniel's help the little girl's life would have been unbearable.

What started as a childhood friendship developed into a deep relationship. Daniel was good to Christina and they visited each other's houses to play. As the friendship grew, both Ruby and Auntie Mag tried to stop it. Ruby, because she regarded Christina as some one of a lower class, and Auntie Mag because of a deep secret which she kept to her breast.

40
THE COURTSHIP

Childhood slipped away with ring games and marbles moving slowly into the background. The teenage years appeared but the two young people were too busy studying and succeeding in the three major Jamaica Local Exams to think of any thing else.

As they studied, they grew closer often going to each other's houses and also to the bamboo patch to study together. They became a pair of inseparables. Both became monitors at the school and they decided that their future lay in the classroom. They took turns to do the research from the few textbooks that they possessed and the discussions and conclusions helped them to remember the details of each lesson.

They did the third Jamaica local and both passed with honours. The whole village joined in the congratulations and celebrations. The school Principal and other teachers were proud. It was a rare thing in both that village and the others around them that two people had passed with honours

In order to get into college to be trained as teachers, they had to pass the entrance exams and go to interviews.. It meant studying again. Christina would go to Bethlehem Teachers college in the countryside of St Bess and Daniel would go to the city to Mico Teachers College.

They both succeeded in each of the entry requirements and then the problem of separation from each other began to haunt them. Could one do without the other in the wide open world out here? Christina, in particular, was frightened. Cloistered as she was in the Revival compound with the people she had grown up with and then the open space of the village that she had been used to, began to be a haven. Could she escape it? Could she do without Daniel who had helped her overcome the shame of being called devil pickney?

Daniel experienced sleepless nights. Long Dan sometimes looked at the nineteen year old son with fear. Would he get her in the family way? The rules of being a teacher were strict. He could be kicked out of college and even as a qualified teacher in the classroom for bringing disgrace to the profession. He watched Daniel like a hawk.

Ruby was easier on her son. It was growing pains she often said, but she sat him down herself and told him the facts of life. She had borne Long Dan three more children in the preceding years and she was very much in control of them all.

It was time for Daniel and Christina to confront the truth. Theirs was not just a friendship, it went deeper than that. Daniel decided that as the man in the picture, he had to make the first move. But how? It was a delicate situation. He decided to write her a letter expressing his undying love. He wrote the letter and posted it and the postmistress looked at the name and address in wonderment.

Christina received the letter the very next day. As the letter requested they were to meet on Saturday afternoon in the bamboo patch. It was a place they had favoured as their meeting place during those long hours of study.

Christina dressed carefully. Daniel wore a new shirt that he had received to take to Mico and they met, shy and almost afraid. It was Daniel who spoke first.

"Christina, I can't do without you."

" I can't do without you either," said the girl, almost in tears, happy tears.

They ran towards each other and hugged, holding each other tight. Then both lovers experienced their first real kiss.

"Daniel I love you so much."

"I love you too Christina. Let's get married after college."

"Yes. Yes of course. Come let's tell our parents the good news."

And the two lovebirds walked hand in hand down the road to Auntie Mag past the new chapel that had been built to house the worshippers at Auntie Mag's place and into the compound that Christina knew so well.

Auntie Mag was scattering cracked corn to feed the chickens that swirled around her.

"Cu Cu," she intoned as if she loved every single chicken in the place. Then she looked up and saw the lovebirds holding hands and her face went grim.

"What have we here?" she asked, her voice low and menacing.

"We want to get married Mama, after College."

"You want to what?"

"Get married Mama," said Christina wondering what she had done wrong. The young people stood in the yard amongst the chickens in fear, what had they done wrong?

Auntie Mag emerged with a brand new dress, a revival style head dress and a pair of garden boots. She came and pulled their hands apart. Then she put Daniel to the right of her and Christina to the left. "Come!" she said, "we walking like this to your father's house," and so they marched down the road past the bamboo patch and into the yard where Daniel lived.

41
REVELATION

"Auntie Mag mad bout something. Wonder if her daughter pregnant?"

Various versions of that was the conversation as the three person marched down the road. Daniel was puzzled and Christina was close to tears.

They walked to the front door of Long Dan's house. It was a Saturday so the whole family would most likely be at home. Auntie Mag knocked three times and flustered Ruby came to the door, opened it and said "What have we here? Daniel, what have you done?"

"Nothing Mama."

Auntie Mag hissed her teeth. "I want you, Long Dan and the three of us in the front room now right now." Her voice was so loud that Long Dan, who was in the backyard cutting the hedge rushed in. The helper who was in the kitchen frying dumplings looked on and proceeded to the best place to listen to the drama. They met in the living room and Auntie Mag motioned for all five to sit down while she held the place captive as she had done from the pulpit these many years.

"These two young people want to get married, but it cannot happen. It would be a case of incest."

"Incest Maggie? You gone mad or what?" Long Dan shouted at her.

Maggie's voice was low now almost a whisper. "Christina, you cannot marry Daniel, Daniel is your brother."

Ruby jumped up in fury.

"Dan!" she screamed, "Explain this. What did you do and when?"

"I did no such thing. I never touched this woman. Maggie what are you talking about?"

Auntie Mag smiled, innocent as a babe. "Dan knew nothing about it. I raped him as he slept."

"Rape? How come?"

I gave him something to sleep in stew peas and he ate it and went to sleep while you went to St Bess to visit your mother. I got pregnant and got my beloved daughter Christina. Dan, you are Christina father. These two young people cannot marry."

Christina looked as if she was in shock. She stood and pointing a finger at her mother, she shouted.

"Mama you lied you lied to me. Who was George Milton? Who was he? You are no longer my mother. I am leaving this place now never to return. You lying conniving woman you you?" With that she burst into tears and rushed to open the front door pushing the listening helper out of the way.

Dan sat with his head in his hands. His world had fallen around him. Daniel went quietly to his room lay on the bed and cried.

Ruby took charge. She hugged her husband. "You will get over this," she said quietly.

Then she went to her son who looked shell shocked.

"Mama," he said, "why Mama why? We were so happy." Auntie Mag left the house and walked down the road to her house. Christina was already gone. She had taken the cardboard grip that she had packed to go to the college, she took the money from its hiding place and walked rapidly away, far away. Mad Ants and Tall Blacks saw her go and wondered why. No one in the district ever saw Christina again. It was as though she had vanished from the face of the earth . By evening the whole village knew the news flew into every nook and cranny of the place.

42
AFTERMATH

After a month or two of rumours and carry go bring comes, lies and counter lies mockery and derision, the village settled to its old slow moving pace. Long Dan consulted the new pastor who was Jamaican, about his plight and was comforted by prayers and promotion in the church . Daniel went off to Mico hopeful that this whole episode would be forgotten and he could return home for holidays . Ruby became the perfect wife and mother, teaching Sunday school and helping her husband to adjust to his new reality, a man who had been raped by a woman, who had fathered a child without being aware of it. The tattle tale helper was fired and Ruby's children though not so aware of what had transpired, soon adjusted and soon forgot all about it..

Auntie Mag suffered for far into the year but her stern, strong self came to the fore and her church prospered. Both men and women came to hear her sermons which were full of under-standing of the Jamaican situation. She preached forgiveness and the importance of loving one another. She became a philanthropist of sorts, providing back to school equipment and some cash to needy children.

Mad Ants and Tall Blacks also prospered as did their wives and off spring. The two men beat the drums and their wives sang and played the tambourines to the joy of the growing congregation. As the other church lost people to Auntie Mag's , a very thoughtful man who had lived in the mother country and had returned to resettle in the village was heard to say " The woman strong she take on the British empire and win."

But in spite of all this, Auntie Mag was lonely and many nights as she went to her bed just before sleep she would be heard to mutter, "Christina. Christina."

ABOUT THE AUTHOR

Jean Goulbourne is a poet, short story writer, novelist, and educator from Cross Keys, Manchester, Jamaica. She worked as an educator in secondary schools and colleges, and was part of the writing team for The Butterfly Series, now known as The Blue Mahoe, a series of books for reluctant adolescent readers. She is also the author of several other books for children published by a variety of Jamaican and British publishers, including her recent young adult story, *When the Bitter Bush Blossoms*.

Her books for adults include the short story collection, *The Parable of the Mangoes*, available through Abeng Press, which (under the title *Caged Birds*) was runner up for the Una Mason prize in 1995, the poetry collections, *Woman Song* and *A New Day*, and a novel, *Excavation*.

Individually, her stories and poems have appeared in *Savacou, Bim, The New Voices, The Caribbean Writer, Nimrod, New Poets of Jamaica, The Literary Review, Focus, Pathways, Dreamrock, Facing the Sea, Caribbean Poetry, Caribbean Poetry Now, New World English, Bite In, Oxford book of Caribbean Poetry, The Daily News, The Jamaica Record, The Jamaica Herald, The Sunday Gleaner, The Sunday Observer Arts Magazine, The Children's Own*, *Scribbles, Metamorphosis, Caribbean Challenge* and other magazines throughout the Caribbean.

9 798822 470368 5